A Dope Boy's Queen 3

Aryanna

Lock Down Publications and Ca$h Presents
A Dope Boy's Queen 3
A Novel by Aryanna

Aryanna

Lock Down Publications
P.O. Box 944
Stockbridge, Ga 30281

Visit our website
www.lockdownpublications.com

Copyright 2021 by Aryanna
A Dope Boy's Queen 3

First Edition September 2021
Printed in the United States of America

Lock Down Publications
Like our page on Facebook: Lock Down Publications @
www.faccbook.com/lockdownpublications.ldp

Book interior design by: **Shawn Walker**
Edited by: **Kiera Northington**

Stay Connected with Us!

Text **LOCKDOWN** to 22828 to stay up-to-date with new releases, sneak peeks, contests and more…

Submission Guideline.

Submit the first three chapters of your completed manuscript to ldpsubmissions@gmail.com, subject line: Your book's title. The manuscript must be in a .doc file and sent as an attachment. The document should be in Times New Roman, double-spaced and in size 12 font. Also, provide your synopsis and full contact information. If sending multiple submissions, they must each be in a separate email.

Have a story but no way to send it electronically? You can still submit to LDP/Ca$h Presents. Send in the first three chapters, written or typed, of your completed manuscript to:

LDP: Submissions Dept
P.O. Box 944
Stockbridge, Ga 30281

DO NOT send original manuscript. Must be a duplicate.

Provide your synopsis and a cover letter containing your full contact information.

Thanks for considering LDP and Ca$h Presents.

Dedication

This book is dedicated to Sheila aka Daddy Lia. The love that grows daily is one of my biggest blessings. I love you, Lil One.

Acknowledgments

I heard them saying that Aryanna ain't got IT no more. That the pen dry and the skills are washed. LMAO. NEVER WILL I QUIT THIS SHIT OR DISSAPOINT! If this is what you wanted, then hold on because I got more heat that you need. God blessed me, so here's my gift to you.

Thank you to every single person who helps me on a daily basis. I couldn't be who I am without you being who you are.

Shout out to my G-wall fam: B Havoc, JBoy, Buckshot (Mosby's own), Nitty from the City and the DRIP QUEEN, Debo, King (The Shine), and the whole STONE NATION. I love all you crazy mufu*kas! If I forgot anyone, that's my bad, but you know what the time limit is on the kiosk. LMAO. #FREEDAGUYS

LDP! We still here and ain't going nowhere!

Aryanna

CHAPTER 1

The feeling of blood flying made me open my eyes, and the look on Mo's face said it all. When she hit her knees, she looked up at me, and opened her mouth. No words came out though, just a rush of blood cascading down her succulent lips and over her chin. When her eyes closed, I knew death had taken her, and that released the paralyzing hold she'd had on me since she'd pointed her gun at me.

"Fatz!" I said, scrambling to his side where he was laid on the ground.

I took the gun from his hand and put it on the ground while I inspected his wound.

"It's-it's ok, it went straight through my shoulder," he said, grimacing in pain.

"I thought…when you pulled your gun, I thought—" —

"I'd never hurt you, Claudette…and I couldn't let you get hurt because of my decision to have sex with you."

I could see the truth behind the pain in his eyes, but I didn't know how to feel about it.

"Is-is Mo…"

He couldn't bring himself to ask the question, and I couldn't verbalize the ugly truth, so I simply nodded my head. He closed his eyes and bowed his head, but that didn't take away his pain's visibility. Even though I'd literally been here for every moment of what had just transpired, I still had no fucking idea how shit had gone so bad so fast. My best friend and the woman I loved was laying behind me dead, and I was trying to stop the bleeding of the man who'd killed her.

Part of me felt like at the very least I should've been avenging her death, but how could I? Fatz had killed the woman he loved to save me. It didn't make sense, but then again, nothing did right now.

"Come on, we gotta get you some help," I said, helping him to his feet.

"No hospitals, Snow. We've got too much heat, and too many enemies for that right now."

"It's ok, I've got a doctor friend I can call," I said, picking up his gun.

I could feel myself wanting to turn around and look at Mo, but we both refrained from doing that as we headed back towards the house. Once we got inside, I helped him to the couch, and then I ran to get some towels to help stop the bleeding.

"I got it, just call your friend," he said, accepting the towels from me.

I pulled my phone out and made the call to Kevin. I wasn't trying to explain over the phone, and he didn't ask any questions, other than what equipment he needed. After I told him he needed to sew, we disconnected our call, and I turned my attention back on Fatz.

"I don't have any pain medication because as you know the house is new, but I can get you a little something to take the edge off," I offered.

He actually smiled at me before shaking his head.

"The bullet hole doesn't hurt compared to…I mean, I know what I'm feeling now will never go away, and it shouldn't."

"That's not a pain or guilt you'll ever carry alone." I said softly, sitting on the couch next to him.

We sat there side by side in silence, both trapped in our own thoughts, until the doorbell chimed. I hurried to answer the door and let Kevin in.

"He's in the living room, straight down the hall and to the right," I said, stepping aside.

Kevin moved past me into the house, but I didn't follow him. Instead, I accepted what had to be done next was on me. I walked outside and approached Mo's body slowly while trying to gather the necessary courage. It took me several deep breaths before I could get close enough to put my arms under her and lift her so I could drag her away. I could feel the tears sliding down my face as clearly as I could feel the warmth still radiating from her body. I had to push all emotions to the side though and focus on what had to be done. I dragged her body to my Lamborghini, and quickly put her in the trunk.

My next move was to find a water hose so I could spray the blood off the driveway. When that was taken care of, I went back inside and sat quietly in the corner, while Kevin handled his business. I was trying to figure out what my next move was, but my mind kept going back to the body in my trunk. It wasn't just anybody, it was Mo. She was part of my spine, part of my chemical makeup and the air I'd breathed for more years than I could remember. The future was just so hard to see without her in it, and yet I knew I had to if I wanted the rest of my family to survive.

"I'm giving you a prescription for some Oxy's to help with the pain. You need to use your left arm as little as possible because it'll hurt more if you rip those stitches, and I've gotta redo them."

"I got you, Doc, and thank you," Fatz said.

Kevin packed his shit, and I walked him back outside.

"Listen, Claudette, I don't know exactly what's going on, but I know it ain't good. I know you're a good person though, and for that reason, I hope you make it out of this in one piece."

"Me too, Doc. Me too," I replied seriously.

He gave me a quick hug before getting in his car and leaving just as quietly as he'd come. I went back in the house

11

to find Fatz sitting in the exact same spot I'd left him in. For a moment we didn't speak, we simply stared at each other. Even though I was only across the room from him, it felt like there was an ocean between us.

"What do we do, Snow?"

"There's no easy answer to that…so to be honest, I don't know."

"Of course you do, you're Claudette Snow, and you can't forget that," he said, staring at me hard.

I absorbed his statement, while forcing my mind to mentally switch gears so survival was at the forefront.

"We're at war, and what happened couldn't have come at a worse time. I feel truly alone right now," I admitted.

"You're not alone though, so what do we do?"

"Regroup," I said.

He nodded his head in acceptance of this answer, but I still didn't know where to begin. Mo's death was sure to shake my team, and the facts of how it went down were sure to make some of them question my ability to lead. Questions like that were what led to mutiny, and that wasn't an option. So, for now that only left one option.

"We've gotta move," I said.

"Ok, where are we going?"

"I don't know. All I know is we're not in any condition to go to war with the cartel. With Mo gone there's a hole, and not just in our hearts. I don't know how we explain this shit to any of our people, and I honestly don't want to. So, we leave," I said.

"Snow, it doesn't sound like you're talking about leaving or moving. You're talking about vanishing."

I thought about what he was saying, and how much sense it made. There was no part of me that was a bitch, but if I was nothing else, I was a smart bitch. Fighting a war I couldn't win made about as much sense as committing suicide.

"Ohhhh shit," I said softly.

"What? What is it?"

"You just gave me the best idea with what you said. The best way for someone to stop looking for you, is if they know they can't find you. Nobody looks for dead people," I said.

The questioning look that he gave me was comical, but I knew if I gave him a minute that he'd figure out where I was going with this.

"So, we're gonna fake our deaths?"

"And then we're gonna vanish," I replied.

Aryanna

CHAPTER 2

Ten Years Later

"Zion, come get your shit out of my damn living room."

"Alright, Ma, I'm coming," he hollered back.

"One day, I'm just gonna throw his shit out in the street, and him with it," I vowed.

"Who are you lying to, Snow? You know *damn well* you ain't gonna do nothing like that to that boy."

The look I turned on Fatz shut his lips, but the smile that lingered made me want to smack him anyway.

"Ma, is dinner done yet?"

"Did I *call you* for dinner, Asad?" I asked.

"My bad," he said, raising his hands high, and backing out of the kitchen.

"Bae, what's wrong?" Fatz asked, moving to stand behind me, while putting his hands on my shoulders.

I was about to shake him off, but I thought better of it. I didn't have a real reason for the anger I was feeling, but I was feeling it, nonetheless.

"I'm good."

"Snow, you're *far* from good right now, so talk to me," he said, turning me around to face him.

I could feel my frustration boiling to the surface, but I forced it down because I didn't wanna fight.

"I told you I'm fine, Fatz. It's nothing."

"It's *not* nothing, now talk to me," he insisted.

I'd hoped the exasperated breath I let out would force him to drop the subject, but the look on his dark chocolate face was one of determination.

"I'm sorry about my bag and books being on the floor," Zion Junior said, coming into the kitchen and kissing me on the cheek.

I started to smack him upside his head, but he was giving me that smile he knew I hated. It was his daddy's smile, and Junior had inherited it, along with his dad's muscular build. Asad had the same build, same smile, and same mean streak as both his brother and father, but he was more conscious about cleaning up after himself.

"Aww, nigga, you just sucking up because your birthday is tomorrow," Asad said, laughing as he came back in the kitchen eating some candy.

Fatz heard this of course, and that made him look at me with understanding now. He'd been with me long enough to know that Junior's birthday was always a hard day for me, no matter how long it had been since my ex had died. I didn't love Zion anymore, but I'd be lying if I said I'd forgotten the fact that him and our son shared the same birthday. It was hard to forget the man who had single-handedly shaped my life like he was God in heaven.

"I don't gotta suck up because it's my birthday weekend, I'm just apologizing because I was wrong," Junior said.

The look on his face was so sincere it made all of us laugh, which I knew was his motive all along.

"Boy, shut the hell up and help your brother set the table," I said.

Neither of them made me repeat myself, but despite the laughter we'd shared, Fatz still had a concerned look on his face.

"Everything is gonna be alright, bae. We've been here before, and we always get through it," he assured me.

How did I explain that this year was different, even though I had no idea *why* it was different? I felt like I was gonna sound like a crazy person, and I was damn near feeling like one. I knew I could trust my nigga to hear me out though.

"Something is different, Fatz. I can't explain it, and nothing has happened to justify the bad vibes I've got, but I can't shake this shit. I just feel like something *bad* is coming."

"One thing I've learned since meeting you, is that you've got better instincts than anybody I've ever met. So, all you have to do is tell me what you wanna do, and I won't ask you why. I'm with you always," he said, placing a gentle kiss on my forehead.

I smiled up at him, knowing how lucky I was to have this good man, after all I'd been through. The sacrifices he'd made for me in the last decade were beyond measurement, and the one he'd made that put us together was one neither of us could forget. Fatz had been my definition of real from the moment we'd met, and I knew it wasn't in him to change.

The last day my life had taken a catastrophic change was when Fatz had killed my best friend, who was his girlfriend, to save my life. That moment had bonded us in a way only blood can and from there, the journey had been on. In that moment we'd made the decision to give up everything we knew for the uncertainty of a future together. I had no regrets, because we'd found peace and created that same thing for our kids. I just wasn't feeling that peace right now.

"Honestly, I don't know what I wanna do. Maybe we just need a vacation," I replied.

"Oooo, can we go back to Colorado, or somewhere else where it snows?" Alexia asked, breezing into the kitchen and going to the refrigerator.

"Suddenly you don't like the weather in sunny Dubai, Miss Bourgeois?" Asad asked.

"I love the weather, but I haven't gotten to snowboard in *years*. Besides, Colorado holds good memories for me," she replied.

I caught the smile her and Junior were sharing, and it still caused my stomach to drop after all these years.

"You realize they're adults, right?" Fatz whispered to me.

"He's still my baby, and I warned you I'd kick your ass if she corrupted him."

"I corrupted her, mom," Junior said, smiling devilishly.

Alexia giggled and looked at Junior with all the love in her eyes that's reserved for young hearts. I hadn't really expected them *not* to fall for each other considering that they'd been practically together since they were kids, but he was still my son.

"Just remember the rules of my house," I said, looking at both of them.

"Do you *honestly* believe they ain't fucking, Ma?" Asad asked.

"Bruh, shut the fuck up," Junior said seriously.

Asad simply laughed, while putting his hands up like he didn't want no smoke. Before I could say anything, Fatz had his lips pressed to my ear, whispering some shit that had me blushing instantly. I chuckled and gave him a quick kiss before turning back to finish dinner.

I didn't hear Junior say anything, but the sound of him smacking his brother upside the head echoed around the room. I snickered, and I could hear Alexia trying to suppress her laughter.

"Five minutes," I announced, turning off the pot of rice on the stove.

Fatz moved to start taking dishes to the table, while I put the finishing touches and seasoning on the beef stir fry. When I was satisfied, I brought the main course to the table, and sat down. Once everyone was seated, I nodded towards Alexia, and she led us in prayer.

Listening to her speak had me reflecting on all the lives that had been ruined or changed because of my quest to be a queen pin. My dreams of being the modern-day Griselda Blanco had fucked up each of these children's lives and stolen their innocence. I'd thought I was doing right by honoring my husband's memory, but hindsight taught me that he hadn't deserved that type of loyalty. Every night I laid awake, asking God to tell me how I could fix this. How I could somehow give my kids a good life, and an opportunity to be all they wanted to be. I believed in the power of prayer, but God sure did take his sweet ass time.

"So, Mom, are we really going on vacation?" Asad asked.

"I don't know. I guess I'm just feeling out of sorts because of Junior's birthday," I admitted.

I immediately felt Fatz take hold of my hand and give it a reassuring squeeze.

"Mom, we don't gotta celebrate my birthday this year. I'm twenty now, and you've given me *great* birthdays my entire life, but I'm good now," Junior said.

"Besides, we should be more focused on the baby shower," Asad said.

My mind had been travelling the past, into all the birthday experiences I'd managed to give all three of them during our life on the run, so what Asad had said didn't immediately register. I thought I'd misheard him, but the silence accompanied by the stares from everyone erased my doubts.

"Who-whose baby shower?" I asked weakly.

"Mine," Alexia replied meekly.

My eyes shot towards Fatz to see if he was hearing the same thing as me, but his body was a blur because he was already moving. Before I could get a word out of my mouth,

Fatz had his hand wrapped around Junior's throat, and he was lifting him out of the chair.

"Dad!" Alexia screamed, jumping up.

"Easy, Fatz. I like you, but you're about to fuck that up," Asad said, tapping him in the back of the head with the .357 snub-nosed pistol.

Right about now, I was happy as hell I'd taught all my kids to shoot and given them guns. At least I was, until Alexia pulled her pink, pearl-handled .45 revolver out and pointed it at Asad.

"If you shoot my dad, I'm shooting you, I promise."

"You better shoot to kill because we're all gonna die in this bitch," Asad said.

"*Stop it! All of you!*" I yelled, hopping to my feet.

"Fatz, put Junior down, and you two put your fucking guns away, before I shoot everybody and eat this food myself," I threatened.

Everyone was slow to move, but they eventually complied with my demands.

"Fatz, come here," I said.

I could feel the fury rolling off of him like summer heat waves, but he let Junior go, and came to stand beside me. It was on the tip of my tongue to tell him that he couldn't even be mad after all the times he'd told me to leave the kids alone. Leaving them alone had turned us into grandparents, but I thought better of shooting an *I told you so* right now.

"Alexia, are you *sure* you're pregnant?" I asked.

"I mean, I haven't been to the doctor or anything, but I've taken at least twelve pregnancy tests in the last week, and I ain't had my period in two months."

"*Two months*? Why the fuck didn't you say something?" Fatz asked in a hostile tone.

"Because I was scared," Alexia admitted.

20

I could tell by the look on Fatz's face that her words had softened him a little, but we still had a long way to go.

"Baby, you don't gotta be scared of me, I'm your dad and I love you no matter what."

"Oh, I know that, Daddy. I'm scared of Snow," Alexia stated, cutting her eyes at me.

I opened my mouth to ask her why she was scared of me, and then I remembered they weren't the innocent ten-year-olds anymore. They knew I had a body count, and we weren't talking about sex partners.

"Alexia, you don't gotta be scared of me, sweetheart. I love you like you're my own daughter, and I thought you would know that by now."

"I do know that... I just didn't know how you feel about abortions," she replied.

"Wh-what? You wanna have an *abortion?*" Fatz asked in disbelief."

"Hell no!" Junior said.

"We didn't know if *you* would want me to have an abortion," she clarified.

I walked around the table and stopped in front of her.

"Sweetheart, I would *never* make that decision for you. I'm not God and that's between you and him."

She smiled brightly before stepping into my arms and hugging me fiercely. The look on Fatz's face was definitely indecisive as to whether to be happy or not, but I knew him. He would *never* leave his daughter for dead.

"Now come on, let's eat before the food gets cold," I said, kissing Alexia on the cheek, while leading her to the seat beside me.

I could tell Fatz still wanted some smoke, but he took a seat and stared flames at Junior instead.

"Ma, pass the beef," Asad said, smiling with the devilish innocence he'd mastered.

The conversation was strained, and the sound of forks hitting plates had never been so loud in my life. The melodic ringing of the doorbell sounded like a five-alarm fire going off, and all the kids scrambled at once to get it. I took the brief moment alone to turn to Fatz and see if I could smooth any of his ruffled feathers.

"They love each other, bae."

"But she's my little girl," he replied emotionally.

"That may be, but she ain't been little in a while, and—"

The sudden sounds of gunshots echoed throughout the entire penthouse, halting my words. Fatz and I jumped up at the same time and sprinted from the room in the direction of the shots. I came around the corner and skidded to a stop at the sight before me. Junior was on his back with Alexia hovering over him, her hands pressed against the bleeding wound in his chest.

"God, no," I mumbled, moving to my son's side.

"Lexy, what happened?" Fatz asked.

"I-I don't know. He opened the door, and the gunshot took him off his feet," she replied, crying.

"Where's Asad?" I asked.

"He went after whoever shot Junior," she replied.

I looked to Fatz, and no words were necessary. He grabbed Alexia's gun off the floor and headed out into the hallway. I could hear shots being fired, but my attention was on Junior.

"Ok, son, you're gonna be fine."

"This-this shit *hurts*, Mom."

"I know, baby, but it's gonna be ok. I promise," I said, wiping my tears away.

"Wh-why is it so cold?" he asked weakly.

"No, Junior, don't do that. *Don't* say that!" Alexia moaned, crying harder.

I could feel the vomit stirring in my stomach as the prayers ran through my mind at light speed.

"I love- love you, Lexy," Junior said, coughing up blood.

"Oh, my God, *please*! Junior *please*!" she sobbed uncontrollably, pressing harder on his wound.

I felt frozen, like I was watching a movie I desperately wanted to turn off, but I couldn't. My mind raced with options of what to do, but the nagging question of *who* had shot my son was interrupting my train of thought. I had a lot of enemies, but I had to know exactly which one had finally caught up to me before my next move was made.

"Keep the pressure on it," I said, scrambling to my feet and rushing to the phone on the wall.

I punched two buttons, and a face came up.

"Yes, Ms. Snow?"

"Send the resident medic to my penthouse immediately and lock the building down. We've got intruders."

Aryanna

CHAPTER 3

"M-Mom?"

"I'm right here, Junior," I said, squeezing his hand as the tears continued their journey down my face.

"Am I going to a hospital?" he asked.

"No baby, we're gonna take care of you right here," I said, squeezing his hand again while watching the doctor search for the bullet hole.

"Wipe," the doctor instructed.

Alexia immediately wiped the blood that was steadily leaking from right over top of Junior's left nipple. He almost crushed my hand when he squeezed it, but I didn't care, because it meant he was still alive and kicking.

"Fuck!" Junior growled, when Doctor Njame used his scalpel to cut around the bullet wound.

The doctor's hands were steady and moved with confidence, as he traded the scalpel for the tweezers that allowed him to get inside the wound and grab the bullet.

"Hold him down," Njame said.

Fatz took hold of Junior's shoulders, and I grabbed his arm.

"Ahhhhhh!" Junior screamed, bucking against the hold we had on him.

"It's ok, son, it's ok," I said, holding him tighter.

I could feel every muscle in his body flexing angrily, but his heartbeat was strong.

"Almost got it," Njame said, with a look of pure concentration riding his face.

"Hurry up," Junior growled.

I could tell the moment the doctor grabbed the bullet because Junior went deathly still, and then his spine defied gravity.

"Asad!" I yelled.

Seconds later, he came into the room and jumped right into the fray. With all of us holding him down the doctor was able to successfully remove the 9mm slug. He put the bullet on the floor next to his medical bag, and then he quickly moved on to the next part.

"Do you want something for the pain before I sew you up?" Doctor Njame asked.

Junior was in too much pain, so he nodded his head vigorously. Doctor Njame reached into his bag and came out with a needle. I started to ask some questions, but before a word could get past my tongue, he'd popped the top off the needle and swiftly injected Junior. I waited with bated breath for a few moments to see if the medication would help. It took a full minute before Junior's body relaxed somewhat, and he looked up at me with relief in his eyes.

"Sew him up, Doc," I said, holding his head while running my fingers through his short dreadlocks.

He'd never looked more like his father than at this moment, laying here in my lap bleeding. My mind travelled back to the times I'd had to nurse Zion back to health from various wounds. I'd had the strength just by using my willpower to get him back to a hundred percent, and I'd do the same thing for our son now. A knock at the door stopped everybody from moving except for the doctor.

"Fatz, you answer it. Alexia, you and Asad go into the back bedroom, and stay there until I call for you," I instructed.

Everyone moved and I pulled my own gun out to protect myself and Junior, should the shooting start again.

"Who is it?" Fatz asked.

"Security!"

I heard the sounds of the alarm deactivating so that the barrier could raise, and then the door was opened. As an owner of the penthouse, I was afforded all the security options that came with the purchase of my property. As a paranoid dope girl, I'd made upgrades to the standard, which was why a full lockdown meant my house was a fortress.

The shooting had triggered a personal lockdown of my penthouse that rivaled the movie *The Purge*. My windows were already bulletproof, should a bullet find its way that high up, but now those windows were hidden behind impenetrable Teflon. The front door was protected by a transparent barrier made by NASA engineers, and it could withstand an explosion of up to ten pounds of dynamite.

The personnel in the building that made up the security detail were all ex-Special Forces, or equivalent to the CIA. When money wasn't an option, you could get the best hittas the world had to offer, but having all of this at my disposal still hadn't kept my son safe. That was my only concern now.

"Ms. Snow, we caught the shooter," Manuel said, coming into the room in front of Fatz.

"Where is he?" I asked.

"In the basement being looked at by another doctor. He attempted to take some type of pill when we cornered him, but we pumped his stomach before it could take effect."

"Keep him alive until I get down there," I said.

Manuel gave me a curt nod before turning around and leaving. Fatz followed him out, and once I heard the security system reactivate, I laid my gun down.

"You're gonna be ok, sweetie," I said, leaning down and kissing his cheek.

"I'm sleepy, Mom," he whispered, fighting to keep his eyes open.

"You're safe, son. Go to sleep," Fatz said, putting his hand on my shoulder.

I looked up to find him standing over the two of us. The compassion in his eyes warmed my heart, but the animal pacing back and forth in him reinforced the venom in my veins.

"Done," Doctor Njame announced, backing away from Junior while taking his gloves off.

"I got him," Fatz said, passing me his gun.

I moved back so he could scoop down, and pick Junior up. My son wasn't a small man by any means, but his six-foot, two hundred and forty pounds was lifted with ease. Fatz was still the same height from when we'd met, but his somewhat chunky frame had been transformed because of his interaction with my sons. They all worked out together, pushing each other to their individual goals of fitness.

Alexia and I worked out together so we could keep up, but watching Fatz lift Junior like he was a sack of feathers, let me know he was on a different level. I could feel his power even though he wasn't touching me, because it was directly tied to his anger. The waves of rage rolling off of him fed the lioness in me that was pacing as well, and I was embracing it.

"How bad is it, Doc?" I asked, once Fatz had carried Junior from the room.

"He's lucky, because a few centimeters lower and it's his heart that stops the bullet. He should make a full recovery as long as you give him the proper medication."

"Bill me accordingly," I said, extending my hand in thanks.

"He'll receive the first dose within the hour. The shot that I gave him won't hinder the healing process at all, but it will allow him to rest comfortably."

I nodded my head in understanding, while silently thanking God for all the medical advancements in the world today. The medicine the doctor would prescribe for Junior would have his bullet wound healed completely within thirty-six hours. Normally, this medicine was only available to the military, or for *extreme* situations cleared by the government, but money could buy anything, and I had money.

"Thanks again, Doc," I said, showing him to the door.

When he was gone, I leaned my back against the door, and opened my mind. It had been a while since I had to mentally go full-battle mode, but the ugly truth was, it felt good. I felt reinvigorated, and ready to remind the world of who Claudette Snow was.

"Mom?"

I opened my eyes to find Asad standing in front of me, with his gunmetal gray Draco-74 clutched in his hand.

"What is it?"

"Are we gonna go handle the people who did this?" he asked.

The look in his eyes reminded me of his daddy so much, but it also reminded me of his mom. I hated Phillisa with a passion that hadn't dissipated any in the last ten years, but that hadn't affected my love for Asad. I loved him for who he was, and because he was Zion's son. I knew he had the blood of a killer in his veins, and I tried not to encourage that, but I damn sure wasn't about to let him be ignorant on how the world worked.

"I'm gonna handle it," I replied.

"You taught us that family protects family. Am I a part of this family, Mom?"

"Asad, you know you are, and you know I love you, but—"

"But *what*, Mom? You've raised us to be who we are, so are you now gonna try and shelter us?" he asked.

"Asad is right, Mama Snow. Ever since we had to go into hiding, you've taught us everything we needed to know in order to survive. Did you do that thinking we'd never have to apply it?" Alexia asked, coming to stand beside Asad.

"Honestly, I *hoped* you'd never have to apply it. I wanted you to maintain your innocence for as long as you possibly could," I replied.

"The day you explained to me that my mother wasn't coming home again, was the day the last of my innocence was taken. You know when the first part of it was snatched from me," Asad said, lifting his T-shirt so I could see the scars from him being shot.

A five-year-old had no business being touched by violence, but Asad had been, and he'd survived to remember it. I knew this contributed to his want for vengeance, as much as the fact that he'd had to grow up without both of his biological parents. None of these kids had a normal life, so there was no reason this conversation taking place should've surprised me.

"What's going on?" Fatz asked, coming around the corner and stopping behind Alexia.

"We wanna go downstairs with Snow and handle the muthafucka that shot Junior," Alexia stated.

Fatz's eyes met mine and they held compassion, entwined with understanding. This was the life we'd chosen for ourselves, but we'd tried to choose better for our kids. Had we failed them? Or had the curtain been necessarily pulled back on the magic act the world had orchestrated?

"The time to take the leash off of you all will happen sooner than any of us wanted, but now ain't that time. Right now, I need you two to guard Junior, and get ready to move. Pack light, and only take what's absolutely necessary," I said.

"We're really leaving?" Asad asked.

"You tell me. What's the smartest move going forward, and what did we learn today?" Fatz asked.

For a moment no one spoke, but I could see the wheels spinning in Asad's mind. He glanced at Alexia briefly, and she gave him a subtle nod.

"The first move has to be to find out who came after us, and it makes sense to move because whoever it is, obviously knows where we are. We learned our location has been compromised... so we have to assume *every part* of our lives has been compromised. We can only trust each other," Asad replied.

"And that's the way it's always been," I said, looking directly at him.

He nodded before turning and heading in the direction of Junior's room.

"I'll lock the door behind you," Alexia said.

Fatz moved past her and opened the front door so we could leave. I checked the clip in my gun before stepping in the hallway, and he did the same thing.

"So, what do you think?" he asked, once we were in the elevator going down.

"I'm not sure what to think, honestly. I've anticipated this day and dreaded it all at the same time. I *never* wanted the kids to be a part of this, but the look on their faces told me I couldn't get them out of it, had I wanted to. We raised them to be able to take care of themselves, and we just ran into what that looks like."

"It's a scary feeling to look at your kid and see yourself," he said.

I could tell by his facial expression he'd been unprepared to meet the woman his little girl had morphed into. Finding out she was pregnant was a big enough pill to swallow, so I knew he could've done without seeing the look of a killer in her. None of it could be undone though.

We rode down to the lobby, and then switched to a service elevator so we could move two floors below that. When the door opened on our destination, Manuel was there to greet us.

"Right this way, Ms. Snow."

He led us down the hall to a door with no markings on it, and let us in. The minute that the door opened, I heard blood chilling screams, and they were as beautiful as Alicia Keys serenading while playing the piano. Manuel led us past two people, sitting at different computer terminals working steadfast, and down a short hallway to another door. When this door was opened, I came face-to-face with a naked man tied to a chair, badly beaten, but very much alive. The stocky man of Middle Eastern descent who'd been delivering the ass whooping took a step back and let me approach the prisoner.

"This is the man who shot your son," Manuel said.

My mind shut off all emotions, which allowed me to step into the old me.

"Who sent you?" I asked calmly.

No response was given, but I hadn't really expected one.

"Last time I'm going to ask. Who sent you after my family?" I asked.

The man coughed up a huge glob of blood and spit it at my feet. I didn't pay it any attention when I looked down, I simply took aim at one foot, and put two holes in it. I never gave his screams time to get comfortable in the air before I put the barrel to his right kneecap, and pulled the trigger. Now his screams were taking on a slight hysteria, but I knew he still wouldn't talk. I put the gun in his lap and let the heat from the still smoking barrel scorch his nuts.

"Who sent you?" I asked, with the same amount of calm.

His mumblings would've sounded unintelligible to most people, but I made out just enough of his broken English to have what I needed. I put the gun to the head of his dick and pulled the trigger. His most prized possession split open like a dollar hot dog from 7-Eleven, causing the other men in the room to moan sympathetically.

"Let him bleed out," I said, putting my gun away and turning for the door.

"Y-yes, ma'am," Manuel replied.

We were led back out of the room and five minutes later, Fatz and I were riding back up to the penthouse.

"Did I hear him right?" Fatz asked.

"What did you hear?"

"It sounded like he said Zion was after you," he replied.

"Then you heard him clearly."

"Ok, but Snow, that's *impossible*... right?"

"Right. Zion is definitely dead," I said.

"So, then what the fuck is going on?"

"Whoever it is was just sending a message. My past is back to haunt me."

Aryanna

CHAPTER 4

"Baby, talk to me. I know you're not sleep, and you've been lying beside me for hours now without saying anything."

"What do you want me to say, Fatz?"

"Snow, you've *never* shut me out, so all I'm saying is don't do it now. You know I'm here, and I'm in this shit with you until time no longer exists."

I could hear the frustration in his voice, but it didn't overpower the sincerity. Fatz was battle tested, built on bloodshed, and definitely hood approved, so I wasn't worried about whether or not he would fold. He wouldn't.

The thoughts haunting me right now were strictly about the unknown. I had more enemies in the world than Jesus of Nazareth, and not enough eyes to see everything that was coming. How did I fight what I couldn't see? How did I protect my family from a ghost?

"I'm not trying to shut you out, bae, I'm still trying to process what's happening," I said, turning on my side to face him.

"Do you have an idea of who it might be?"

"No...I just know it could be anybody or everybody," I replied.

"But what is your gut telling you?"

I stared at him hard for a moment, trying to work up the nerve to utter what was unspoken between us.

"Phillisa," I whispered.

He didn't say anything, and the only light in the room was courtesy of the moon, but the lack of surprise was still clearly visible. I'd had a feeling that the moment he'd heard my ex-husband's name, his mind had offered up the most obvious suspect. I hadn't spoken it before now though, for the same reason he hadn't. Neither of us wanted *that* bitch to be the devil knocking at our door.

"Do you really think she's somehow managed to track us down?" he asked.

"Do you know anyone else who would still be so motivated to destroy me after a whole decade?"

"I mean, you did *a lot* of dirt, Snow, so we can't exactly rule other enemies out."

"That sounds plausible, but you asked for my gut feeling, and my gut tells me Zion's other baby mama is out there in the darkness."

"If that's true, then we've got *more* than a problem," he said, breathing heavily.

"Now you understand why I haven't said shit."

He nodded sadly before pulling me into his arms. I rested my head on his chest and took comfort in the fact that I had him here to lean on. Phillisa wasn't just out to kill me, she wanted to erase me from history's books. The feeling was definitely mutual, because the blame for everything wrong in my life could be placed squarely on *that* bitch's shoulders.

Had she *not* fucked my husband, *and* gotten pregnant by him, then her father wouldn't have killed him. I wouldn't have been caught in the web of that same sick, sadistic muthafucka who'd spawned her, and been forced to forever blur the lines of good and evil. I would be a normal housewife, baking cookies and cakes for the church fundraiser, or some shit like that. But I wasn't that woman, and Phillisa was the catalyst for what had become my life. She wished death on me, but I wished she'd never known life.

When Fatz and I had hatched the plan to vanish ten years ago, I knew she would scour the earth for her son. I'd been able to produce dead bodies and fake dental records for me and Fatz, but there hadn't been time to fake the kid's death.

At the time, I'd felt like the pain of not knowing whether her son was dead or alive was the icing on the cake, and it couldn't have happened to a nicer person.

But as the years passed, and I experienced all the joys of raising Asad as my own son, I realized I'd more than likely created a monster when it came to Phillisa. I'd taken her reason for living, and given her a purpose God himself couldn't have talked her out of. I'd brought the devil to life, and the blood of my own son was now on my hands.

"What am I gonna do if he finds out she's alive?"

"There's nothing you can do except to tell him the truth. The question is do we do that now, later, or never?" he replied.

"I vote for never."

"Me too...but the only way that's gonna work is if we find her, and kill her first," he said.

"I know."

What I didn't know was how the hell we were gonna kill a goddamn ghost. I had been keeping tabs on Phillisa as best as I could without her getting wind of it, but five years ago, she'd fallen off the grid. It had been wishful thinking to hope death had come for her, but I had been almost convinced that it had. In hindsight, that could've caused me to let my guard down, which had resulted in Junior almost losing his life. Now the churning in my stomach told me Phillisa was back, and she wasn't about to play nice.

"What do you want to do, baby?"

"Right now, I want you to take my mind off of all of this shit," I confessed.

He needed no more prompting before he rolled onto his back and pulled me on top of him. My face was inches from his, as I stared deeply into his dark brown eyes. Trust wasn't a question, and neither was love or loyalty. I was honestly beginning to see if I could see the end. I knew in every fiber of my being this man would ride with me until the bitter end, but I wanted to know if he felt like this was it.

"Until my heart stops beating, I'll stand by you, Claudette, no questions asked."

"I love you."

"I love you too, baby," he replied, pulling my mouth to him.

Our kiss contained the hunger and fire of the uncertainty surrounding life. My hands went to his dreads, as his slowly caressed my back and ass. The harnessed strength of his touch always made my pussy throb, and I felt the familiar thumping immediately. One of the things I loved most about our intimate moments was that he knew what I wanted and needed without having to be told. He took his time, kissing me with passion and patience. He made me feel like a high school girl again, because even though we knew the destination, he let it be known there's no rush.

I straddled him, but I didn't take his dick inside me yet. The feeling of him throbbing against my thigh made me smile, as I sucked on his bottom lip teasingly. I could feel his body temperature rise instantly, which forced mine to keep up. When his hands went to my own dreads and pulled so my neck was exposed to him, I took a deep breath. His tongue moved with a painter's precision and detail, causing goose bumps to manifest on my skin.

I reached down in between us and took the head of his dick inside me. The response to me squeezing him gently with my pussy muscles was a moan that rumbled from deep in his throat. I took that as my welcome invitation to start my slow descent on him. The feeling of his dick filling me up had me hypnotized like I was in a trance, but I kept moving with patience. The slow rocking motion pushed him deep within my walls and had us throbbing together in no time.

His grip on my hair tightened, as he pulled like my mane held the power to increase my speed. I fought the urge to break out in a full gallop and maintained the slow wind I was working with my hips. His sexual fury was fast building, and barely harnessed, if the way he was lifting his hips to meet mine was any indication.

"Love-love me, bae," I mumbled, moving a little faster.

"Always, Claudette."

I could feel the truth in his words as he rolled me over until he was on top of me. Passion flared when he plunged his hard dick back inside the heat of my wet pussy and started fucking me like he missed me. Despite the padding of our headboard, my head still felt every jarring blow that came with the delivery of dick. There were no fucks given though, and I proved this by locking my legs around his back. The look in his eyes was almost completely predatory, like I was a shark, but he was a megalodon. I knew no fear, only love, and that allowed me to stare him down as he tried to destroy me.

I opened my mouth to cry out, but he timed his deep dives so that he knocked the wind out of me with each blow. The buildup of my climax was blindingly fast, and before I knew it, I was clinging to him as reality faded.

"F-f-fuck!" I screamed, digging my nails into his back.

He bit down into my shoulder at the same time and moments later, I felt his cum flood me. The feeling of his body shuddering with mine only intensified the aftershocks, and the fact that he kept fucking me slowly had me seeing stars on the backs of my eyelids.

When I'd regained my composure, I rolled him back onto his back and jumped back on the dick with determination. We spent the hours until sunrise battling for dominance in the bedroom, but we ended up calling it a draw before we killed each other.

"One of these d-days, I'm gonna bend you to m-my will," I panted, fighting to catch my breath.

"Please do," he replied, smiling as he pulled me to him so we could spoon.

Before his sweat could dry on my skin, I could feel the need for sleep tugging at me like an insistent child. I gave in without a fight or second thought, falling fast and hard into my slumber. The feeling of waking came too soon, but the moment my eyes opened, I knew instinctively we had to move.

I reached behind me to wake Fatz up, but all I felt was the coolness of our silk sheets. I hopped up so fast that my head spun for a few seconds, forcing me to lean on the bed.

"Fatz!" I called out.

Seconds later, I heard footsteps, and then he came around the corner fast.

"You ok?" he asked, moving swiftly to my side.

"I'm good. How is Junior? Where are the kids?"

"He's fine, and they're fine. We've been waiting on you to wake up," he replied, easing me back down on the bed.

"Why, what's wrong?"

"Nothing is wrong, except for everything that's wrong. We were waiting for you to wake up so we can leave," he said.

I looked at him closely to see if he could possibly be concealing anything from me, but I didn't detect any deceit.

"Ok, I've gotta make arrangements to get us out of Dubai quietly, but we still have to decide where we're going," I said.

"I've already made the arrangements, and the kids took a vote on where we're going."

"A vote? Who the fuck told them they had a right to vote?" I asked, with rising anger.

"Snow, calm down. The kids ain't exactly babies anymore, so it's only right they get a say in how their lives play out."

"That's bullshit because it's *us* that has to keep them safe!" I said, getting back to my feet and putting my finger in his face.

"I know you better calm the fuck down."

His tone was low, but the threat was easy to hear. Fatz wasn't the abusive type, but he was a man that would tell anyone that put hands on him, they better know how to fight. I didn't take a step back because I wasn't scared, but I did put my hand down.

"Just for curiosity's sake, where did they pick to go?" I asked.

"Back to the United States."

My initial reaction was so bad I literally bit my tongue, but I took that as a sign to think before speaking.

"Did you explain to them the unsurmountable danger that awaits us back in the United States?" I asked.

"Don't talk to me like I'm stupid, Claudette, because you know I'm not, and neither are the kids for that matter. The reality is that there's danger no matter where we are, and that's obvious by the bullet wounds Junior is recovering from. So, their logic is that it's safer to have home court advantage. I tried to argue that you wouldn't listen to that logic, but it might change their minds hearing it from you," he said, stepping aside as she gestured for him to lead the way out of the room.

I could hear the underlying sarcasm, but that only served to piss me off more and push my buttons. I immediately stormed from the room and went in search of the kids.

"Everyone in the living room *now*!" I demanded, loudly. I could hear movement coming down the hall, but I resisted the urge to scream for them to hurry up. Asad came around the corner first, followed closely by Alexia.

"Have you two lost your damn mind?" I asked, before they could take a seat.

"No, but you *clearly* feel like we have," Alexia replied.

I could tell by the way she angled in front of Asad she was gonna be doing the talking. If she thought I wouldn't pop her ass in the mouth because she was carrying my grandchild, then she had me fucked up.

"Going back to the U.S. is like committing suicide, and I *know* you silly muthafuckas ain't trying to die," I said.

"No, we're not trying to die, and that's why it's safer to go home. You and my dad were two people *nobody* wanted to fuck with, Snow! So, we all have a better chance at surviving if you two reclaim the throne. Everybody knows home court advantage can make or break a game, and if we're gonna be in a fight for our lives, then we want *all* the advantages we can get."

"Ok, so let's say we do go back. Have you forgotten your dad and I abandoned *all* the people who had our backs? We don't have an army anymore, Alexia, and if we did, what makes you think they would fight for us?"

"Because I know how you and my dad think, Snow, which means that the people on your team would understand your decisions. You put your children's lives first, and *no one* is gonna blame you for that," she stated confidently.

"I can't gamble with your lives, Alexia, nor the life of my grandchild. I don't want that blood on my hands."

"Would that blood not be on your hands if we got killed somewhere else? The bottom line is that you ain't God, so you can't stop the inevitable. What you can do is minimize the risk," she reasoned.

I opened my mouth to continue with the same argument, but I saw Fatz step into the living room and he wasn't alone.

"She's right, Mom, and you know that. I know you love us and want to protect us, but right now you gotta stop thinking like a mom. You have to think like Claudette Snow," Junior said.

I wanted to use his weakened state as a reason to argue against what he was saying, but he was staring at me the same way his father used to. Only a fool argued with the truth, and Zion never hesitated to remind me of that way back when.

I looked to Fatz, who was supporting Junior's weight with his shoulder. The look in his eyes told me he'd back my play no matter what, but he agreed with the kids. I didn't know whether they were all crazy, or if I was the only sane one in the room, but I wanted to choke the shit out of *everybody*! I felt like none of them understood what they were asking of me.

It was one thing to play with the lions, but it was another thing to try and make one a pet, because then it would do more than chase you. It would devour you if you weren't moving fast enough.

"Are you all sure?" I asked, looking around.

"We are, Mama Snow. I wouldn't bet my child's life on anyone but you, so believe me when I tell you we talked about this extensively."

"Ok then. Everybody get ready to leave. We're going home," I said.

Aryanna

CHAPTER 5

Ten Days Later

Norfolk, Virginia

"Ball up, nigga."

"Come on, Gunz, that wasn't even no foul!"

"I said, *ball-up*!" Red Gunz repeated, taking his place at the top of the key on the basketball court.

It was obvious the man holding the ball didn't wanna give it up, but the furtive looks he was throwing around spoke to his fear. Every ghetto in America operated under the same principles, and one of the cardinal rules was never let *anyone* see fear.

If I could see it from my position perched on the hood of my Maybach coupe, then I was sure the niggas on the court could too.

"Bruh, I didn't foul you," the light-skinned nigga holding the ball said.

Gunz didn't speak again, he simply held his hand out for the ball. The nigga holding it took one more look around, and then he turned his back to Gunz. He didn't say shit else, he just kicked the ball over the fence. I couldn't hear what he was mumbling as the ball flew, but the next actions told me what was about to go down.

Gunz kept his hand out, but instead of getting the ball one of his homies stepped forward and passed him a pistol. The sound of the first round being chambered echoed loudly across the blacktop, forcing everyone to stop moving. That included the nigga who'd just ended the game with his bullshit.

"Come on, Gunz, it's just a basketball game," the man said, holding his hands straight up in the air.

A young woman suddenly sprinted onto the court and skidded to a stop in front of the man with the gun being pointed at him.

"P-please, Gunz, he didn't mean to disrespect you," the woman begged.

Red Gunz still didn't utter a word, but I could see the look in his eyes, in between the long red tipped dreads swinging in his face. I could tell by the way his muscular frame was taunt, just what was going through Gunz's mind, because I'd seen his mind at work years ago. He was the very definition of a killer, and the bad news for the couple in his pistol's sights was that he *enjoyed* being that way.

"Gunz, please, I'm begging—"

The woman's final plea was silenced by the loud crack of the first shot being let off from the deadly Sig Sauer .45 Gunz was holding. The man standing behind her never got to utter the first word of his plea, because the second and third shots had his name and DNA on them. The gunshots didn't affect anyone on the court, or on the sideline, but the sound of the bodies dropping made people run faster than most Olympic track stars.

In the chaos it was easy to identify Gunz's people, because they calmly gathered around him and escorted him off the blacktop. I got up off the hood of my car, preparing to go have a word with him before he left and possibly went underground, but the feeling of Fatz's hand on my elbow stopped me.

"Not here, bae. Get in the car."

I knew Red Gunz through Fatz, so I knew I needed to listen to him with regard to handling this situation. What I wasn't about to do though was get in the car and take cover, while my man stayed exposed to deal with what one could only assume would be a hostile reunion.

"What are you gonna do?" I asked.

"Just arrange a sit down, that's all."

"Ok, well, I'll wait for you right here," I said, leaning back against my car, while crossing my arms over my chest.

I could immediately tell Fatz wanted to physically put me in the car, but too much time would be wasted fighting a battle he couldn't win. He shook his head as he turned and headed in the direction of the line of black SUVs that obviously belonged to Red Gunz's army.

Before Fatz could get all the way up on him, he was stopped by two soldiers. Gunz barely spared a glance at first, but when he recognized the ghost from his past, he stopped dead in his tracks. Gunz made his way over to Fatz and looked him up, and down, before pulling him into a fierce embrace. They hugged like only men can and then the sound of sirens broke up the reunion.

I could see Fatz was trying to extract himself smoothly, but Gunz was having none of that. Before I could intercede, he was pulling Fatz with him towards one of the trucks and they disappeared into the back. I was able to lock eyes with Fatz before he was out of sight, and there was no panic there. I didn't know what else to do, other than to follow my man, so I quickly got behind the wheel of my car.

Seconds later, the motorcade moved out, and I was on their ass. They moved through the city of Norfolk with a familiarity I lacked, which made it hard to tail them without being noticed. I pulled it off though, and when they turned into an apartment complex half an hour later, I eased to a stop at the curb around the corner.

I double checked to make sure my HK fully-automatic 9mm pistol was fully loaded, before I tucked it into the waist of my shorts and pulled my shirt down over it.

I ran through the same check on the Draco in my purse, and made sure extra clips were in there too. I got out, set the alarm on the car, and walked away like I belonged there. I had no idea where I was going, but I knew I didn't like the layout of these projects. There was only one way in, and there were no lookouts visible.

Some people might think that was a good thing, but I knew the lack of human cameras meant there was *plenty* of high-tech surveillance being used. Controlling real estate looked a lot different than how Nino Brown and G Money had done it in *New Jack City*.

I walked into the neighborhood casually, but my eyes were scanning everything at lightning speed. I didn't see any of the SUVs, so I kept walking deeper into the trenches. I felt like there were a million eyes on me, and there probably were, but I kept my cool. I'd been in different hoods all around the world, so I knew as long as I moved like I was supposed to be here, then there wouldn't be a problem.

It took almost ten minutes for me to walk to the very back of the projects, and that's exactly where I found the SUVs. There was a row of five identical buildings, but not a soul was posted up outside to give me any hints. I pulled out my phone, and dialed Fatz's number. When it rang only twice before going to voicemail, I immediately hung up and called right back. This time it went straight to voicemail, and that only served to piss me off. I shot Fatz a text message that told him he was on thin ice, and he better tell me where the fuck he was.

I waited the longest five minutes of my life, and then I contemplated my next move. I tried to fight the impulsiveness I was feeling, but I lost that battle almost instantly. As my fingers tapped with bullet speed, I quickly climbed up on the hood of one of the SUVs and sat down. I started a slow thirty-count in my mind, but I only got to ten before two big, dark skinned niggas appeared out of the last building on my left, headed in my direction. I fired off one more text message before I put my phone in my pocket and sat my purse in my lap.

"Ay, get the fuck off my truck!"

"I wanna go for a ride," I said with fake excitement.

"Bitch, you better get off that goddamn truck before I give you a ride on a bullet!"

Based on the anger displayed by both men, I could tell it was gonna take more than some fake flirting to get what I was after.

"If you take me for a ride, I'll suck both of your dicks *and* I'll swallow the cum," I said, smiling devilishly.

My statement caused both men to miss a step like the concrete was uneven, and they bumped into each other to keep from falling. The laughter that rolled out of my mouth was genuine, and I couldn't stop it. They regained their composure, and I looked away for a few seconds to let them get their swag right.

"We'll give you a ride. Where do you wanna go?" the taller of the two asked.

"Anywhere we can be alone, and smoke a blunt," I replied.

"Well, if that's all you want, you should just come up to our spot with us."

I made sure to fix an expression of uncertainty on my face as I looked from one man to the other, but not in a way that said I was shutting down.

"Is it just you two in the apartment?" I asked.

"Why, do you want more action than that?" the other man asked.

I gave them my sexiest smile while getting down off of the truck.

"Only if you two can't handle little ole me," I replied.

"Oh, we can handle you right, Dre?"

"Damn right, Leroy. Let's get back to the building before the boss sends someone out here to confiscate this pretty, young thing," Dre said, looking over his shoulder as if someone was coming.

Leroy offered me his hand like he was a perfect gentleman and not the nigga who was just threatening to shoot me. I took his hand, and that put him first in line to die in my mind. When Dre smacked me on the ass as I passed him, I knew I would enjoy his death equally.

I was led into the apartment building, and up to the top floor, like a lamb to the slaughter. Their minds were working overtime just imagining all the freaky shit they were about to do to my big booty, cute ass, but mine was formulating my plan of attack. As soon as we walked into the apartment, the smell of good weed hit me in the mouth, and had my sweet tooth jumping.

"Damn, it smells *amazing* in here," I said, spinning around like a little girl in a toy store.

"We had just sparked one before you interrupted us," Leroy said.

"You ain't mad at me, are you?" I asked, seductively.

"Don't worry about it, baby, you can make it up to me."

"She can make it up to *both* of us," Dre corrected quickly.

"Well damn, if y'all bout to have a party, then I'm in too."

The new voice in the room caused me to cease spinning immediately and lock in on the woman approaching. At first glance, you might've mistaken her for a nigga, but I'd heard just enough femininity to know she had a pussy like me. The swag made it clear she wanted the same thing these niggas did, but I knew that only made her more dangerous, because she could think like me too.

I evaluated her, from the tops of her golden-brown dreadlocks, down to the Gucci sneakers she was rocking. There was obvious intelligence in the light brown eyes, as well as good natured humor, but neither of those things hid what I was looking for. The windows to her soul revealed a killer just below the surface. This probably should've made me nervous, considering I was operating on foreign soil, but it had the opposite effect by making my pussy wet.

"And you are?" I asked.

"You can call me Ace," she replied, taking my hand in hers.

I thought she was gonna pull it to her lips and kiss it like they did in old school movies, but she did something slicker. She held onto it. If this was an ordinary situation, these niggas would have realized they'd just been outmaneuvered by this five-four, hundred-and-ninety-pound-gangstress. I could look at her and tell she was all trouble, all the time.

"I like your accent...it's Jersey, right?" I asked.

"What you know 'bout Jersey?" she asked, surprised, yet pleased.

"I'm far from local, so I've been through your area," I replied.

She smiled, and I could tell she was about to say something, but suddenly a weird look came over her face. I knew what it was instantly. It was recognition.

"Hold up, Ace, she's *our* guest," Dre said, putting a protective arm around my shoulders.

"Where'd you meet her?" she asked, letting my hand go, but still locking eyes with me.

"Don't worry 'bout all that. We'll let you know if they're growing a field of fine chocolate bunnies, and then you can pick out your own," Dre replied, steering me towards the couch.

I sat down and crossed my legs slowly, while looking up at Ace. I saw clearly with the knowledge recognition brought, there was now indecision swimming in those sexy eyes of hers. There was an unspoken decision that had to be made, and I was comfortable letting her make it.

She stared at me silently for a few moments as the fellas made preparations around us for the threesome that would never happen. The moment the light went out in her eyes, I knew her decision had been made, and I was ready.

"What are you doing here, Mrs. Snow?" Ace asked.

"Hold up, you *know* this bitch?" Dre asked, looking between the two of us.

"I know *of* her...and so do you," Ace replied.

"Ok, so you know her, big deal. You can fuck her after we've had our turns, now move the fuck around," Leroy said, impatiently.

Ace didn't move, nor did she really pay Leroy any attention. She was waiting on my next move, and I liked that.

"My dude is here somewhere with Red Gunz, and I need to know where," I explained.

Me mentioning Gunz's name got both niggas' attention and just like that, quick sex wasn't the only thing occupying the space in between their ears.

"Wait, who the fuck are you to be speaking Red Gunz's name?" Dre asked, aggressively grabbing my arm.

I smiled before looking at him, because their attention was so focused on me, they'd forgotten Ace was even in the room. A pretty chrome .45 Smith & Wesson pistol materialized in her hand, and a loud cough from the barrel stopped Leroy's thought process. The bang of the gun going off made Dre jump, and he made the mistake of taking his eyes off of me.

My hand darted in my purse with a snake's swiftness, and it came out clutching my pearl-handled straight razor. He never got to make a move, before I flicked it open and severed the carotid artery in his throat. While he flopped around on the couch trying to keep his blood from running like a river, I stood up to address Ace.

"It's been more than a decade since anyone has seen me...so how did you know who I was, Ace?"

"Because I ain't local either and you're a legend in the game. I never thought I would actually *meet* you though, especially since you're supposed to be dead."

I stuck the razor in my bra and extended my hand to her.

"Now you've met the ghost, the myth, and the legend. You can call me Snow," I said.

"You're sexier in person."

"We'll save that conversation for another time, if you don't mind. Right now, I need to know where Gunz has my nigga," I said.

"He's probably in the next building over, but there's no way to sneak up on him, so I hope you've got a plan."

"Well, I've always been a direct person, so my approach has always been to just go knock on a nigga's door," I replied.

She looked at me like I was crazy, and I could tell she was tempted to laugh, but my expression remained deadly serious.

"Kn-knock on the door?" she asked.

"Absolutely. The devil always knocks because there's always a sucka on the other side to answer."

Aryanna

CHAPTER 6

Ace threw me one more questioning look over her shoulder, and when she saw my expression wasn't changing, she shook her head in disbelief before knocking on the door. I leaned up against the wall next to her with a bored expression on my face, waiting patiently. On the inside I had the old feeling of butterflies in my stomach before a killing, but I didn't let it show in any way.

"Who is it?" a deep voice called out.

"It's Ace, and my bitch. I need to see my cousin."

The revelation of Gunz being her cousin had gone unmentioned until this very moment, and for a split second I considered the very real possibility I'd been crossed. My weapons gave me a feeling of security, but two guns compared to whatever I was about to walk into was like having a butter knife.

When Ace looked at me, I knew she could read my thoughts, but she smiled reassuringly before taking my hand in hers again. A few seconds later, the sound of locks being turned echoed loudly throughout the stairway, and I knew it was too late to back out. The door was pulled open by a huge light-skinned nigga with a bald head, and more tattoos than hairs on his arms.

"What up, Hook?" Ace asked.

"Not shit, Ace, but I think Gunz is busy right now. Some shit jumped off at the basketball court, plus he rolled in with some new nigga, so I don't know if he'll see you right now."

"Trust me, he'll see me because I'm bout that paper, and there's nothing that nigga loves more," Ace replied.

"Except pussy," Hook said, looking pointedly at me.

"Easy big fella, she's spoken for," Ace said, pushing her way inside the apartment while pulling me behind her.

I followed her lead, making sure to keep my eyes low but observant, nonetheless. There were several niggas spread out around the living room, playing video games, and listening to music.

"What up, Ace, where you been?" a short, fat, brown-skinned dude asked, while passing her a lit blunt.

"Out handling business, you know how it go, Popeye. What you niggas getting into?"

"Shit, we 'bout to crank up this dice game in a minute. You want in?" he asked.

She took two healthy pulls on the blunt before passing it to me.

"Nah, I gotta handle some business with cuzzo really quick, but I'll get wit' it later."

I hit the blunt with enough force to stress my lungs, like swallowing a gallon of water, and passed it back to Popeye.

"Aye, he said he didn't wanna be disturbed," Popeye said, holding his hand up to stop our forward progression.

"Bruh, you already know I'm that nigga *favorite* cousin and besides, do you wanna be the one to explain to him how he missed out on a business opportunity?" Ace asked.

I could see the indecision on his face, and I knew we had him.

"Don't tell him I let you back there though," Popeye said, stepping aside.

"You know I got you, my nigga."

He nodded his head and we moved past him, deeper into the apartment. As we neared the back bedroom, I could hear voices raised, and that made the hairs on the back of my neck stand up. Ace looked back at me, and I nodded at her to go ahead and knock on the door. She did, but there was no immediate response, and the voices didn't lower any. I stepped around her and hammered on the door like I was the

ATF. There was immediate silence, and then the door was snatched open. I didn't blink at the sight of the gun inches away from my face.

"Damn, two ghosts in one day. Where the fuck are them *Ripley's Believe-It-Or-Not* muthafuckas when you need them?" Red Gunz asked.

I stared him dead in the eyes until we had an understanding, and then I pushed the gun aside so I could step into the room.

"What are you doing here, bae?" Fatz asked, hopping up off the couch.

He'd moved fast, but not fast enough for me to misunderstand the intentions of the white bitch who'd been sitting on his lap.

"Bae?" Gunz asked.

"Aww shit," Ace said, from behind me.

"I was worried about you, but I see you all good," I replied, staring at the white girl.

I could tell she was smart enough to keep her mouth shut, but Gunz should've told her smiling wasn't good either.

"Why wouldn't he be good, Snow? It's not every day one of my niggas comes back from the dead," Gunz said.

I turned to look at him, and I saw Ace shaking her head out the corner of my eye.

"It's good to see you, Gunz," I said, holstering my attitude.

"You too, El Jefe. How do you and my cousin know each other? Or do I even wanna know?"

"Shut up, fool, and put that damn gun away before I tell my momma," Ace said, coming all the way into the room and closing the door.

The familiar sound of Gunz's laughter filled the room and instantly defused the obvious tension. I turned my attention back on Fatz, and sent him a look that let him know his ass was sleeping on the couch for a long while.

"Why didn't you answer my calls, Fatz?" I asked.

"Because nobody is allowed to use a phone in my spot. I ain't paranoid or nothing, I'm just careful," Gunz said, making his way to the couch and sitting down.

The white girl immediately jumped in his lap, which told me how free she was when it came to close personal space.

"There was no need to worry, Snow, we were just catching up," Fatz said, coming over to stand in front of me.

"You didn't mention you're in a relationship with the lovely, but dead, Claudette Snow," Gunz said.

"That's probably because we didn't come for relationship advice," I replied sarcastically.

Gunz chuckled, but my attention was focused on my man and the look he was giving me. He pulled me into his arms and put his lips right up against my ear.

"I'm sorry I worried you. And the only reason she was sitting on my lap was because Gunz told her to. I would never play you, baby."

I nodded my head and pulled back so he could see I was cool.

"So, Fatz tells me you're back... but you don't wanna be," Gunz said.

"That's one way to sum it up, but this ain't a conversation we're about to have in front of everybody," I replied, looking at him pointedly.

"Jen, go in the other room," Gunz said, gently pushing her off of his lap.

Ace opened the door for her, and then locked it once she passed through.

"How's your son?" Gunz asked.

"He healed nicely, but it was too close for comfort," I replied.

"Do you know who's coming for you?" Gunz asked.

"The theory we're working with, it's Phillisa," Fatz said.

"Nah, she's dead."

I looked at Fatz before turning my gaze back on Gunz.

"You say that with absolution in your voice, my nigga," Fatz said.

"That's because I'm positive about that fact. Thanks to the dope Snow left behind, I was able to keep business moving. Once the full shipment Phillisa agreed to supply you with came through, I locked everything down like a prison, and since I was the only plug around, it wasn't hard to take over.

"Of course, Phillisa tried to go to war, but she couldn't fight me, J5, *and* Vontrell while trying to find her son. Not even with her Columbian connects, and they were barely supporting her after the fuck shit she did by handing her dad over to you. That shit fucked up some truce she didn't know about between the cartels out there. It took a while but five years ago we got a location on her, and we dropped a bomb on her muthafuckin ass. Literally."

When Fatz looked at me I knew he was thinking the same thing I was, the fact that we'd been unable to track her, starting five years ago. That meant what Gunz was telling us could be the truth.

"Was her death verified?" I asked.

"Verified by who? God? My nigga at the Pentagon hacked a drone for me and turned her compound in Mexico into rubble. There weren't even teeth left to use for dental record confirmation," he replied.

I looked to Fatz again, and he seemed more certain than I was. I knew there was no room for error though.

"Do you remember the mansion, Gunz?" I asked.

"Yeah, what about it?"

"Phillisa's father had that built, and she got to see how useful those underground caves were. So how do you know she didn't use the same tricks when it came to building her own compound?" I reasoned.

"And how do you know this isn't one of your other *multiple* enemies gunning for you? You seem to have a one-track mind, Snow, and that can prevent you from seeing what's obviously in front of you. I know you've heard the saying *you can't see the forest for the trees*."

Gunz had a point and I knew that, but my gut was telling me he was wrong. I didn't know how to convince him of this without insulting him though.

"Alright, so the bottom line is one way or another, we're being hunted by someone highly motivated because we've *been* dead. We can't kill what we can't see, so we need your help to find the person or persons responsible," Fatz said.

"Say less, I've got some connections I can tap into. I advise you to use your connects too, Snow," Gunz said.

"Bruh, any connect we had has probably forgotten about us, and the leverage we had," Fatz said.

I knew Gunz heard him, but his eyes were locked on mine, and he was smiling like a kid with a secret.

"You might wanna ask your girl, my nigga," Gunz said.

When Fatz turned his attention to me, I debated how best to tell him closing your eyes didn't equate to sleeping.

"Snow? What is Gunz talking about?"

"Do you remember when I told you Mo and I had killed the bagman? King Divine? Well, before that happened, I made him give me his black book, which contains all the dirt he had on everybody."

"Ok, who are you talking about, and how valuable is it?" Fatz asked.

"When I say this nigga had dirt on everybody, I mean this muthafucka had dirt on *ev-er-y-body*! The value of that flash drive is priceless."

"Is there a *reason* I'm just now finding out that you've got this type of leverage?" Fatz asked, neutrally.

The sound of Ace snickering wasn't helping any, and I shot her ass a look real quick that shut her up.

"We've never been in a position to need it until now, but just having that ain't gonna be enough. We need people around us we can trust because I *damn* sure ain't bout to trust the people we're about to lean on. Using leverage like this is gonna make us more enemies than friends, because at the end of the day, we're a threat. I would like to fight without that happening, but I understand that might not be realistic," I replied.

"Nah, it ain't, but with the power I've amassed since you've been gone, we're unstoppable," Gunz said.

"I want in," Ace said.

I turned towards her and sized her up.

"What are you bringing to the table besides being a distraction?" I asked.

"Oh, just because I'm a hoe handler, you think that I'm only a distraction. Have you forgotten that sex sells, and pussy runs the world? Or did you just think the bitch who left up out of here was Gunz's bitch?"

"Actually, I did think that was Gunz's bitch," I replied honestly.

"Nah, I run the hoes in these streets, and I've got more where they came from," she said confidently.

"Yo, why are you trying to audition? You my muthafuckin family bitch, and you with me," Gunz said.

I knew she was hearing Gunz, but she was staring me down, waiting. I winked at her before turning back to Gunz.

"So, what's the play?" I asked.

"Where are you and bruh staying, and are the kids safe?"

I looked at Fatz with a question in my eyes, to which he shook his head.

"The kids are with us, and right now we're hiding in plain sight in Virginia Beach," I replied.

"You didn't wanna send the kids somewhere safe?" Gunz asked, looking back and forth between me and Fatz.

"You ain't been around our kids recently," Fatz replied, chuckling.

"I'll take your word for it, bruh. I've got a few different safe houses, and you already know as long as you're with me, you're good anywhere in the seven cities of Virginia. Let me see what the place is to put y'all, and then we can get on the move."

Fatz and I both nodded.

"Can I holla at you for a second, Snow?" Ace asked.

I turned to her and followed her to a corner on the far side of the room.

"What's up?"

"I know you're not the type to trust a bitch off the jump, but I hope you can give me the benefit of the doubt. I know I can learn a lot from you, and I bring my own assets to the table. I'm trying to fuck with you," she said sincerely.

Looking into her sexy eyes was like opening a portal into the past, and I didn't know how ready for that I was. I hadn't fucked with or been around any bitches since Mo and Phillisa, because I didn't know if they were the fucked-up ones, or if I was. I still didn't know the answer to that question, but right now I needed an ally I could count on.

"If you fuck up or try to fuck me over, I'll bury you and your family. Understand?" I asked.

"Say less."

I stuck my hand out and she shook it, but then she tried the same shit she'd done earlier.

"Quit playing," I said, laughing as I untangled my fingers from hers.

"You better *know* I ain't playing."

All I could do was shake my head as I walked back over towards the fellas.

"Alright, you two can have one of my apartment buildings not far from here. Go get your kids, and by the time you get back, I'll have everything set up for you all," Gunz said.

"Thanks, bruh," Fatz said, giving him a quick hug.

"Ace, go with them and take a few niggas with y'all," Gunz said.

"I gotchu, my nigga."

I stepped up to Gunz and wrapped my arms around him.

"It really is good to see you, my nigga," I whispered in his ear.

"Likewise, Snow. Likewise."

I pulled back and smiled up at him before moving back to Fatz' side.

"We'll call you when we're on the way back," Fatz said.

Gunz nodded, and we all turned to leave the room. On the way out of the apartment, Ace pulled out her phone, and I could hear her telling somebody to meet us in the parking lot.

"I need to run back to my apartment really quick. Do you two wanna meet me in the parking lot or come with me?" she asked.

"I need to pee," I said.

"I guess we're following you," Fatz said.

She nodded and led the way back to her spot. I thought we were headed to the same apartment I'd killed two of Gunz's men in, but she led us to the building next to it.

"I just need to grab a few things and we can go," Ace said.

"Where's the bathroom?" I asked.

She pointed towards the back of the apartment, and I headed in that direction. I pissed really quick and I was washing my hands, when I got a feeling that made me look out of the one window in the bathroom. My blood ran cold, and then slowed down as the reptile in me took over. I moved quickly back out into the living room and went straight to Fatz.

"We're being surrounded as we speak."

"By whom?" he asked, pulling his gun out.

"I'm pretty sure it's Gunz's people."

"But why would he—"

Fatz let the question trail off, and I could see the light get brighter in his eyes.

"He thinks you're gonna take everything he's built."

"Or he's lying about Phillisa, and he knows it's her that's after us," I said.

"We gotta get out of here, bae."

I looked towards the bedroom where Ace had disappeared, and I pulled out both of my guns.

"Alright, let me grab some weed really quick, and we can—"

She stopped talking and walking at the same time.

"Why are both of you holding your guns and looking at me like that?" she asked, cautiously.

"We should be asking you why the fuck there is niggas with guns coming from everywhere, headed towards us," I said.

Ace immediately went to the nearest window and peeked out of the blinds. Seconds later, she hit the floor, and the window shattered from gunshots.

"*Muthafucka!*" she growled, pulling her own gun out.

"Are those your cousin's men?" Fatz asked.

"Hell yeah! That dirty nigga set us up!"

I looked at Fatz, and he was staring at me with the same expression I felt on my face. We were in need of another miracle.

Aryanna

CHAPTER 7

"We've gotta get out of this apartment, and down to the basement," Ace said, scooping her bag off of the floor and moving fast towards the door we'd just come through.

Fatz and I followed her out into the hallway, and into the stairway. There were no sounds of footsteps yet, but my heart was beating faster with the anticipation of being run down on. My guns felt light in my hand, but my purse felt heavy on my arm, because I knew it could hinder my movements. I ignored that thought though and ran down the three flights of stairs behind Ace.

Just as we hit the basement level, I heard a door open above us, and those sounds I'd been listening for became a reality. Ace motioned for us to huddle up, and we moved closer to her so we could hear her whispering.

"When I open this door behind me, there are two things that'll happen. The first is an alarm will be triggered, and it's gonna be loud as fuck. Secondly, there are probably some goons waiting on the other side, so shoot without hesitation."

"I'll go first since I've got the automatic firepower," I volunteered.

Ace smiled at me, and then spun around and quickly pushed through the door.

"Crazy bitch," Fatz said, following her lead.

By the time I stepped out into the bright afternoon sunlight, there were bullets on all-go, no whoa. I could feel the smile stretching across my lips, as I raised my guns and let them muthafuckas hunt in the name of the reaper. I saw three faces turn towards me, but they disappeared like smoke in the wind with a tap from both of my triggers. We formed a triangle of sorts and moved in the direction Ace was leading us, while killing with precision.

The problem, other than niggas trying to kill us, was that our transportation was in the opposite direction. Once we'd dropped everybody in our immediate surroundings, we broke out into a sprint towards the fence that kept the projects separated from the outside world. I wasn't in any mood to scale a fucking chain link fence topped with razor wire, but this *was not* the spot where my life ended.

I refused to accept that. I didn't see the hole in the fence until Ace slid to a stop and squeezed her little ass through. Fatz had a more difficult time, which forced me to turn back the way we'd come and be on guard so no one could shoot us in the back.

"Come on, bae," he called a few seconds later.

Two men suddenly rounding the corner with their guns out demanded my undivided attention, and I shot them down immediately. I didn't wait to see if anyone was coming behind them though, I just turned and wiggled my way to freedom.

"We need a car," I said, once I was standing on the other side of the fence.

"Come on," Ace said, taking off at a dead run towards the sounds of traffic in the distance.

We followed her lead again, while keeping our eyes peeled for Gunz's goons. Before we got to the intersection, a gray Dodge Magnum turned the corner in front of us. Ace jumped out into the middle of the street and tried to flag the car down. I could tell by the way whoever was driving didn't decelerate, they had no intention of stopping, and that made me veer off into the street with Ace.

She waved her arms until the car was so close it almost hit her, and then she jumped out of the way. I raised my pistol, and put three bullets through the windshield, which forced the car to come to a screeching halt. Ace wasted no time snatching the driver out of the car, and Fatz wasted even less time putting two bullets in the nigga's head. I hopped in the driver seat and once they'd loaded up, I sped off.

The sight of niggas rushing in our direction with their guns up made me swing the car in a hundred and eighty-degree turn, and I let the Hemi under the hood eat as I smoked the tires while speeding off. I didn't let out a sigh of relief until I saw the first exit that would take us to the highway, and ultimately back to my kids.

"Did-did that really just happen?" Ace asked, breathing heavily.

"Yeah," I replied, feeling the hatred flooding my brain.

"B-but that nigga is my *family*, yo! How the fuck is he gonna do *me* like that?" she asked, clearly hurt by the betrayal.

"If it's any consolation, I don't think that it's personal. You're just not worth more than the little empire that Gunz has built," Fatz said honestly.

"*Fuck that nigga's empire*! Loyalty can't be bought!"

Neither Fatz nor I said anything to that comment because we knew the truth in that statement intimately. On the one hand, it was good to have someone like-minded with us, but I knew it was still a bitter pill for her to swallow. I looked over at Fatz, and the storm I saw raging on his face made my pussy throb.

Red Gunz was a street nigga through and through, but I doubted he understood what the fuck he'd just done. Rule number one when you took a shot at a hitta was you *better not* miss, and he'd fucked that up badly. Not to mention, he'd just made three formidable enemies.

"Are we running from this nigga, because if that's the plan, then you two can just let me out," Ace said.

I looked over at Fatz before shifting my eyes to the rearview mirror.

"We don't run. We regroup," I replied.

The look of fury in her eyes had her ready to insist we go handle this shit *now*, but she kept her mouth shut. We all remained silent for the rest of the hour and a half it took to get back to our hotel room.

"Ace, you can wait right here, we'll be down in a minute," I said.

"Do you want me to get us another car?"

"Nah, just wipe this one down completely, and park it out of sight away from the hotel. Then find the nearest dealership so we can go buy some transportation. We can't afford to get pulled over," Fatz said.

Ace nodded, and we all got out of the car. Despite what Fatz had just said, I still stayed behind to help wipe down the car, and then I let her drive off with it. By the time I made it upstairs, everyone was moving around, getting their shit together. As soon as Junior saw me, he came over to me and scooped me off my feet.

"I'm so glad you're ok, Mom."

"You know it takes more than a double cross to get my old ass."

"I'm by your side from now on, no questions and *no* arguments," he said, staring at me with his daddy's eyes.

"Put me down so we can get the hell out of here."

He reluctantly put me on my feet, and I went to the room Fatz and I shared to get my stuff.

"We've gotta send the kids somewhere," I said, as soon as I walked in.

"That's not a smart idea, bae. No one can protect them like we can, and no one will have our back like them."

"But Alexia's pregnant, Fatz! If something happens...if something happens to our grandchild, I won't be able to live with myself," I said, fighting against the cracking in my voice.

Fatz stopped packing and came to wrap his arms around me.

"Baby, I love all of those children equally, and I will give my life in an instant for them or our next generation. I know how important everyone is, and that's exactly why I can't entrust them to anyone else. We saw what just happened with a nigga I've known for two decades, a nigga we *made*. There's no way I'd trust someone with the lives of our children, baby, and please don't ask me to."

I knew he was right, but it still hurt to be in this position. I nodded my understanding and agreement, and then we both got busy gathering our shit. Ten minutes later, we were walking out of the hotel and meeting up with Ace at the Waffle House restaurant across the street. I let everyone else go in, while I took a lap around the restaurant outside, just to relax my paranoia.

When that was done, I went inside and joined Fatz and Ace at our table. The kids had the table beside ours, but no one was ordering. I knew my children, so I knew they were waiting on an explanation about what had happened, and what was gonna happen next. I sat down and motioned for everybody to get as close as possible so we wouldn't be overheard.

"We've gotta get out of the Tidewater area, because we weren't exactly welcomed with open arms. So now we need to find a place to lay low," I said.

"Colorado," Alexia said immediately.

I started to dismiss her out of hand and tell her to stop living in a childish fantasy, but Junior nodding his head stopped me.

"Mom, she's right. No one knew you sent us there, except for the people you brought with you, so out of those people who do you think would think to look there?"

"I don't know, Junior, but that's risky," I replied.

"I think it's worth the risk. I know you, Mom, and you've *always* done everything you can to protect us. We understand we're your kids, but you can't treat us like kids right now. That means you need to listen to our ideas too."

"The time for arguing about that has come and gone, so from now on we work together," I conceded.

His smile lit up his face for a couple seconds, and then it was back to business.

"So, are we going to Colorado?" Asad asked.

I looked to Fatz to get his opinion, but all he did was nod his head at me.

"Alright, Alexia, I want you to call the airport and rent a jet. Ace, I want you to get us the two fastest cars you can on short notice. We're paying extra too," I said.

"The closest dealership is a Porsche dealership, and from what I'm told, the new 2033 Porsche Cayenne goes zero to a hundred in four seconds flat," Ace said.

"Sounds fast enough," Asad said, smiling.

"Get it done," I said, looking at Ace.

"I'm gonna order some food while we wait," Fatz said, gesturing for the waitress.

"Everybody needs to eat because we're gonna be on the road for a while," I said.

"The airport ain't that far, Mom," Junior replied.

"Do what I'm telling you," I said, pulling out my phone and making a call.

The phone was answered almost immediately on the other end, and I only had two words to speak.

"It's time."

I hung up without waiting for a response, and then I gave the waitress my order. Ten minutes later, we all had our food in front of us, and we were shoveling it in like we hadn't eaten in forever. Once everyone was done, I had Ace call the dealership so they could send a car to get us. An hour later, we were pulling off the lot in two identical, gray Porsche trucks, heading out of town at a brisk pace. It wasn't until we'd left the state of Virginia that Junior called my phone from the truck behind us.

"I thought we were going to the airport, Mom."

"After I just paid a hundred and fifty thousand for the comfort you're riding in? Nah, we're making this trip by land, but I had the jet rented because more than likely, flight plans will be checked. The nigga who tried to kill us is far from stupid."

"Understood. I'm following your lead, Mom."

"Remember those words, baby boy," I said, disconnecting our call.

"Everything good?" Fatz asked.

"Yeah, just Junior needing to micromanage. This whole experience is about to put everything we've taught them to the test."

"Does that worry you?" he asked.

"Not really. Honestly, the only thing that I'm worried about is if it's *that* bitch after us. That won't just rip our world apart, it'll do the same thing to the kids."

"We won't let that happen, no matter *who* the fuck is coming after us," Fatz replied, giving my hand a reassuring squeeze.

The comfort in his touch was scary because it wasn't something that ever got old.

"Uh, I know you two are in charge of this situation, but do you mind if I help since I'm now involved?" Ace asked.

"What did you have in mind?" I replied, turning in my seat to look at her.

"Well, first I need to get that nigga Gunz taken care of, because *nobody* in the family is gonna understand the shit he pulled on me. That should eliminate him as one of your enemies and for that, all I'd ask is you let me take over his territory."

"Do you have the muscle to do that?" I asked.

"A lot of muscle ain't required, just finesse, and I've got that hands down," she replied, smiling.

"That's fine by me, but you gotta make sure that nigga ceases to breathe in a gruesome way," I said.

"I can handle that. You gotta remember I'm from Jersey."

I could see the joy on her face at the thoughts of dismantling a nigga, and it reminded me of Mo a little bit. I didn't know if it was just the fact that Ace was gay, but I was starting to notice I was thinking about Mo a lot more than I had, since stuffing her in the trunk of my car ten years ago.

The weight of that guilt never went away, I just shifted it from shoulder to shoulder so I kinda forgot I was carrying it. Being back in the States was stirring up ghosts and skeletons, but the only way to go through it was to go through it. I meant to see this shit through to the end, and if I was going to hell, then I was taking a *whole lot* of people with me! While Ace got on her phone and made the necessary calls, I sat back in my seat and got on my own phone.

One thing Gunz had done was bring to light that I wasn't fighting as blindly as I'd thought that I was. The world might have thought I was dead, but it was time for the resurrection of Claudette Snow. I'd already reached out to my lawyer friend who had the flash drive from the bagman, so now it was time to see how best to use it. I didn't want to go about my comeback in a legal way. I wanted blood on my hands, and death riding my shoulders.

My first contact was with my old weapons connect and once I convinced him that it was *really* me, I ordered a survival kit worthy of the Russian KGB. I had everything sent ahead to my house in Colorado. Right about now I was patting myself on the back, for maintaining control of all the properties I'd owned, by having the deeds switched to several different corporations within that first year of disappearing.

I really hadn't planned on coming back from the dead, but the lessons Zion had instilled in me died hard. One thing he taught me was to be ten moves ahead if I had any intention of winning the chess game of life. I knew he was probably cussing me out for letting our son get shot, but I was gonna make shit right. It didn't matter what I had to do or who I had to kill, I was hellbent on making things right.

Aryanna

CHAPTER 8

Two days later

Colorado

"Home sweet home!" Alexia cried out happily, running through the snow up to the front door.

Junior was hot on her heels, and before she could get to the door, he had her scooped up in his arms. I had no idea what he whispered to her, but the joy on her face spoke to how happy she was.

"What is it about this place?" I asked, looking over the hood of the truck at Fatz.

"I think it's just the bond they formed here. This probably seemed like the end of the world to them when they were younger, and they made the best of it. They all did," he replied, nodding towards Asad.

When I looked over, I saw an expression on his face that was a mixture of peace and sadness. This was where I'd brought Asad to recover from his gunshot wound, when he was nothing more than a boy. It had been a traumatic experience, but meeting his brother for the first time, and forming a bond with him had made it easier.

Up until that point, Asad had been an only child, so this place symbolized a family outside of the shelter his mother had put around him. This place also was the last place he'd seen his mother alive, because I'd had all of them moved for safety first and then I'd made them disappear for good. There was no doubt this place held bittersweet memories for him.

"Do you think he's ok?" Fatz asked.

"Yeah, he's good. He's a strong kid."

"I've seen snow before, but *damn!*" Ace exclaimed, looking around at the white tipped mountains surrounding us.

"It's beautiful, right?" I asked, taking in the view with her.

"It's gorgeous. If a bitch had to hide out, this is *definitely* the way you do that shit," she replied.

"Well, enjoy it while it lasts, because we won't be sitting by the fire roasting marshmallows. At least not for long," Fatz said.

When I looked at him, I could see the determination written all over his face. I knew he wanted to preserve this world for our kids and grandchild, so there was nothing he wouldn't do. On that, we were in agreement.

"Let's get settled in," I said, heading in the same direction the kids had taken off in.

By the time we got up on the porch, Junior had put Alexia down and realized his retina scan still unlocked the door. When I'd really realized this might've had to be their home for good back then, I'd turned it into their very own fortress. They had access and I had access, but other than that, if a full lockdown was issued, not even Jesus could get inside this muthafucka.

"Mom, she said *yes!*" Junior exclaimed excitedly.

"Yes to what?" I asked confused, looking at him and then her.

When she held out her left hand and I got a look at the ring on her finger, my heart stopped.

"Wh-what are you doing? Where did you get that ring?" I asked shakily.

"It's the ring Dad gave you, and I've had it for years. I knew before you sent me out here that I wanted to marry Alexia one day...so I took it, and I've kept it safe all this time."

His words rendered me speechless, as memories flooded my mind about Zion and our marriage. Zion was definitely a gangsta, but behind closed doors he had been sweet and romantic. He'd given me a new ring every year on our anniversary, and the carats got bigger with each year. The Junior had put on Alexia's finger was the first ring his dad had ever bought for me.

The last time I'd seen it, it was in my jewelry box fifteen years ago. I'd had no idea Junior had swiped it, and now that I did, I wasn't sure how to feel about it. I could feel everyone staring at me, and I knew my mouth was hanging because the wind was rolling rapidly over my tongue. I closed my mouth and swallowed before speaking.

"Are-are you sure, son?" I asked.

"I'm positive, Mom, and I—"

I silenced whatever he was gonna say next by holding up my hand, and slowly walking towards them. I could tell by the way Junior squared his shoulders, he was prepared to battle me about his decision, but I turned my attention to Alexia.

"Claudette," Fatz said.

I could hear his warning for me to keep my calm, just in the way he'd said my name, but I ignored him.

"Alexia, is this what you truly want?" I asked.

"This is what I've dreamed about since I first saw Junior," she confessed genuinely.

I nodded while looking at the truth shining brightly in her eyes. My baby boy had grown up right under my nose, and I didn't like it. I knew it didn't matter what I liked though, because this was *their* life. I held my arms open and motioned for Alexia to give me a hug. She hesitated long enough to look over at Junior and her dad and then she stepped into my hug. I squeezed her and held her as her body shook with tears. I felt my own tears leaking from my eyes and running down my cheeks, but I didn't mind because this was a happy occasion.

"Mom, are you mad?" Junior asked.

I took a step back and turned to him.

"Not at all, son, I love you both."

He quickly scooped up in his powerful arms, and hugged me as tightly as he'd done the day I'd come back to him up here.

"Don't kill her, Junior," Fatz said, laughing.

When he finally put me down, I was out of breath, but laughing as well. We all fell in the house and started discussing when and where to have the ceremony. They wanted it done here at the house, and they wanted it to go down *ASAP*. After the surprise of the baby, and Junior's near-death experience, nothing surprised me or Fatz. The unspoken truth about how short all of our lives might be was the albatross around everyone's necks, but we wouldn't let tomorrow's problems interfere with today. Once we got settled in, the girls took over the kitchen, while the men went to do the shit men do.

"Mama Snow, are you sure you're good with all of this?" Alexia asked.

"Yes, sweetheart. You know I love you, and you're already family. Plus, I know you burn the world for my son and that's a loyalty that can't be bought."

"That's a fact," Ace chimed in.

"I do love that man."

The way her face flushed when she made that declaration almost embarrassed me, but I let it go. The beauty of young love rolled off of her in waves. Despite the fuck shit Zion had done to me and his sons, I knew he was smiling in whatever hell he was burning in.

"I promise to always do right by Junior, Mama Snow. I know it's not easy to give your firstborn to *any* woman, but I swear on the life of our child, I got him," Alexia vowed passionately.

"I've watched you grow up and grow into an amazing woman, Alexia, so I'm good with who my son has chosen. Just know that his ass is *your* headache now."

"Oh, no worries because I *know* how to keep that ass in check," she replied.

We all laughed at that.

"You know, I always wondered what you were like for real," Ace said.

"What do you mean?" I asked, looking up from the pork chops I was preparing to fry.

"I mean everybody in the streets has heard stories of the *ruthless, diabolical*, Claudette Snow. The rumors paint you out to be some sort of monster, so I'd wondered if they were true or false."

"Oh, well, they're *absolutely* true," I said seriously.

For a moment Ace just smiled at me, but I could tell she realized I was being blatantly honest, because the smile on her face evaporated.

"Mama Snow is a sweet and caring woman...but at the same time, she ain't someone you wanna cross for *any* reason," Alexia stated.

Ace nodded her head at what Alexia said, but her eyes remained on mine. There was no fear anywhere within the beauty of her hazel gaze, only lust. I knew why she wanted to fuck me and fuck with me, but I wasn't quite sure why I wanted to do the same things in return. I made a mental note to figure out the answer to that question, sooner than later.

"So, Alexia, are you gonna tell your mom all of the good news?" I asked.

"Do you think it's safe to do that?" she countered.

"Well, you need to touch base with her anyway and let her know what's going on, so that her and your stepdad can be on point," I replied.

"Ok, I'll do that, and I'll tell them everything else too."

I knew despite the distance between Alexia and her mom, they still loved each other very much. It had been hard on both of them to go their separate ways ten years ago, but Fatz had convinced his ex that we'd be able to keep Alexia safe better than she could. In the end Vivianna had made the sacrifice in order to let Alexia live her life and be with the only person she loved. It had crossed my mind to send the kids to Vivianna, but I had no right to put her and her family in jeopardy.

"Yo Lexi, come on, we gotta go," Asad said, coming into the kitchen.

"Go where?" her and I asked in unison.

"Snowboarding," Junior replied, coming into the kitchen behind his brother.

I started to object, but then I made eye contact with Fatz as he came into the kitchen.

"You all couldn't wait, huh?" I asked, chuckling.

"The snow is *calling us,* Mom," Asad said.

"Well by all means, answer the phone, son," I replied, smiling.

"Are you sure, Mama Snow? I don't wanna leave you with all the work cooking."

"You're good, Lexi, Ace will help me," I replied, glancing to my left.

The smile Ace gave me was laced with pure bad intentions, but I didn't mind.

"Make sure all of you take your guns with you," I said.

"Yes, Mom!" the three of them sang together, causing all of us to laugh.

The kids left the kitchen, but Fatz came in and gave me a soft kiss that held so many promises.

"You two play nice," he whispered.

"Shut up, fool," I replied, laughing and pushing him away.

His laughter followed him out of the room.

"Roll up your sleeves and prepare to work, because they're gonna come back *hungry*," I said.

"I got you, but for the record, I think some of the things I've heard about you are bullshit. You're not heartless, you just don't give your heart to everyone, and I can understand that. I've had my heart broken too many times to count, and that shit ain't never been fun."

"That's an understatement," I said.

"I ain't trying to bring up bad memories or anything. I guess I'm just trying to tell you that I see you... the *real* you."

I stopped what I was doing and stared at her for a moment.

"You see me, huh? You sure about that?"

She smiled shyly at me, and then came towards me slowly.

"Yeah, I definitely see you," she said, invading my personal space until our lips were moving in beautiful synchronization.

She tasted like weed and chocolate, which had two of my cravings fulfilled simultaneously. I'd thought I would feel some type of apprehension about being with a woman again, but there wasn't a hint of any mental block. As for my body, the way Ace was kissing me had me on fire from head to toe.

"Your clothes are in the way," she said, pulling my shirt over my head.

I giggled, as I started undressing her too. Within seconds, all we had on were matching expressions of burning desire covering our faces. In the past I would've taken control and had my way with her little ass, but I felt out of touch with my womanly instincts, so I let her drive for the moment. She backed me into the counter and kneeled in front of me, while throwing my right leg up over her shoulder.

The feeling of her tongue flicking across my clit made me grab ahold of her dreadlocks. When she started sucking on it, my head rolled back and my vision got blurry. When she slowly pushed two of her fingers inside my pussy and set a fast rhythm while *still* sucking on my clit, I whimpered without shame. The skill of her tongue, and the way she alternated between licking and sucking me, pulled an orgasm from me within three minutes. I came *loudly*, while gripping her hair with enough force to pull her up into my uterus.

I knew my body well enough to know that once the flood gates were open, there was no turning back. The fact that she was staring up at me with those smoldering hazel eyes only made my climax more breathtaking. I was trying my best to conceal how unprepared I was to get head this good, but I knew that she knew. With every lick I could tell she knew she had me, and she was loving it. I wasn't about to beg though. Not yet anyway.

"W-wait," I panted when she pushed my leg up higher and licked my asshole.

My heart started hammering in my chest like it was trying to outrun me *and* her tongue.

"Oh, *shit*!" I exclaimed, holding on to the counter to give her more access.

She didn't let up with the pressure she was applying with her fingers, nor her mouth and it only took a few minutes before I squirted all over her face. I could barely feel my fingers because I was gripping the countertop so tight, but all I cared about was the dragon she had me chasing. I was too weak to keep my balance, but I still had plenty of fight in me. As soon as my heart rate slowed down a little, I pushed her back, pulled her to her feet and lifted her up on the counter.

"My turn."

CHAPTER 9

Seven Days Later

Norfolk, Virginia

"The arrogance of this nigga is *astounding*," I said, shaking my head as I watched Red Gunz dribble the ball up the basketball court.

He'd killed a nigga and his girl on this same court a little more than a week ago, and here he was back out, playing like shit was sweet. Not to mention, he'd taken a shot at two certified hittas and *missed*! One would've thought he would be scared to show his face for a while, but that assumption was wrong. I wasn't mad though, because it worked to my advantage.

"One thing I know about my cousin is that he thinks he's untouchable. He has always been like that, but he got *me* fucked up this time. My only question is, why didn't you let me have my people handle it? One of my girls could've easily gotten to him and cut his throat while he slept."

I looked over to the passenger seat at Ace and smiled at her, because she'd actually thought she knew the *real me* before today. Now she would see the other way I liked to orgasm.

"This is personal, Ace, and anything personal is handled with our own hands, when possible," Fatz replied from the backseat.

She nodded her head in understanding, before directing her attention back to the basketball game. All eyes were on the action, but at the same time, we were observing the people around Gunz.

"Hey, bae, look up at the second row on the far side of the bleachers," I said, nodding in the direction I was talking about.

"You talking about the two Spanish chicks?" he asked.

"They're Columbian," I said, looking in the rearview mirror at him.

His eyes held the same understanding mine did.

"What am I missing?" Ace asked.

"Nothing, we just know now who we're fighting against," I said.

"Who is it?" Ace asked.

"The woman Gunz said he dropped a bomb on. Her name is Phillisa," Fatz replied.

"The way you all were talking about her that day, I got the impression she was kinda like a big deal. So why would she only have two bitches out here?"

"That's all we see right now, but that don't mean more people ain't lurking," I said.

"So, what's the plan?" she asked, pulling her gun out and chambering a round.

"Easy, cowgirl, we're gonna move when it's smart to move. If Phillisa has people out here then that means she knows we're in the States, and that means she's obviously backing Gunz," I said.

"Or using him as bait," Ace concluded.

What she'd verbalized was the second thought that ran through my mind and had me watching the crowd a little closer. It was a gorgeous day outside, which meant the cute girls were out wearing barely anything, trying to find a baby daddy. There were more niggas than chicks, but seeing the two Columbian females had me watching bitches harder.

"I want you to take in the whole scene, Ace, and tell me what you find weird," I said.

She turned in her seat to get a better look at the basketball court and focused with single-mindedness. My eyes went back to Fatz in the rearview mirror, and I saw he was paying attention to the scene outside our truck too.

"The fact that those Columbian chicks ain't watching the game is weird, because their eyes are on a swivel for something," Ace said.

"What else?" I asked.

She was silent for a couple minutes, with her eyes still trained on the basketball court, before turning to me.

"That's all I see."

"What about you, Fatz?" I asked.

"The gray Range Rover is a 2033 model with autonomous capabilities and it's out of place like shit," he replied.

"Which means, Phillisa or someone high up in her organization is close by. Gunz is touching some paper, but not enough to drop on a two-million-dollar whip," I concluded.

"That's not his truck, I know that for sure," Ace said.

"So, let's see who moves first, because I highly doubt anyone knows we're back in Virginia," Fatz said.

"I doubt Gunz even knows Phillisa has people out here, or that he's the bait. He's just a pawn in her game," I said, while contemplating how I wanted to handle this situation.

It was obvious Gunz was being used to entice us to come out in the open, but the question I had was whether or not Phillisa was anticipating our attack this soon. She might've thought we were running, and she was simply covering her bases in case she was wrong. Or she could've been anticipating an immediate attack because she knew how I thought. There was always a risk when it came to analyzing versus overanalyzing, and that was the fine line I was walking.

"Do you see any of your girls out there, Ace?" I asked.

"A couple, why?"

"Tell them to leave *now*," I replied, pulling my own gun out and checking to make sure it was ready for a meet-and-greet.

I could hear Fatz do the same thing in the backseat, and I could feel a smile touch my lips. I had a feeling he and I were thinking the same thought, and when I looked in the mirror, I saw him smiling at me. We'd been together so long he knew what made my pussy wet.

"Text Junior, bae," I said.

He gave me a nod right before I heard the sounds of his rapid tapping on his phone's screen. Junior and Asad had parked on the other side of the basketball court, so they could come in from the east when we came from the north. This would allow us to hit everybody, without being caught in each other's crossfire.

"They're ready," Fatz said, a few moments later.

"My girls are out of the way."

I looked out the windshield of my truck at the game still in progress and took a mental count of how many people I believed to be armed.

"Start shooting in the bleachers, because that's where the return fire will come from," I said.

No one replied, but they didn't have to. I opened my door and stepped out into the beautiful afternoon sunshine. I hid as much of my MAC-11 behind my back as I could, but I knew the clip was sticking out. When I heard the other two doors slam, I stepped away from the truck, and led the way towards the basketball court. My steps were casual but measured because I didn't see my sons through the crowd yet.

By the time I got to the back of the bleachers closest to me, I could see both Asad and Junior creeping up from the other end. I looked at Ace and Fatz and they moved up to flank me. Once I could clearly see Junior's eyes, I led the way from behind the bleachers with my gun out in front of me.

"Ayo, Gunz, check the ball!" I yelled, smiling as I upped my gun and squeezed the trigger.

Seconds later, the echoing sound of rapid gunfire could be heard, just below the screams coming from across the basketball court. The roar of gunfire on both sides of me made us a mariachi band, and bodies were dropping like roses at our feet. Gunz turned towards his men sitting on the sideline, but before he could take a step, Junior and Asad eliminated them. In the span of twenty seconds, we had turned an afternoon basketball game into a massacre that was sure to make the news in every foreign country. By now, Gunz was laying on the ground, but I knew he wasn't dead. He was only playing possum in hopes we'd leave him.

"Grab him and let's go," I said, turning around in a slow circle to make sure nobody snuck up on us.

Fatz and Ace rushed forward to where Gunz was laying, and Ace hit him over the head with the butt of her pistol. The painful moan that escaped him confirmed the fact that he was still alive like I'd thought. Fatz grabbed his feet, and Ace grabbed his head while we covered them and backed out as quickly as we'd come.

"Be careful," I said to my sons once we'd made it back to my truck.

They both nodded, and then headed towards their ride. I hopped behind the wheel of my truck, and started the engine, but I didn't pull off.

"What are you doing?" Ace asked, turning in the passenger seat to look at me.

"Just waiting to see what the Range Rover does."

"Babe, we gotta *go*," Fatz said insistently.

"We will, just hold up a minute."

I could hear his frustration with my response in the way he took a deep breath, but I still didn't move. It was a long thirty seconds before the autonomous Range Rover came to life, and quickly backed out of the parking space it had been occupying. I dropped my truck into gear and sped towards the other truck.

"*Now* what are you doing?" Fatz asked, sticking his head up in between the driver and passenger seats.

"I'm following this bitch to see where it's going, and *maybe* we can get a bead on Phillisa."

"That's smart, but uh, you *know* we just did some biblical shit, right?" Ace asked.

I spared her a look that made her raise her hands in surrender to my judgement. I turned my attention back to the road and pushed my foot down on the gas pedal.

By the time the Range Rover got to the corner, I was right behind it, sticking to its ass like a bumper sticker. I didn't see anyone behind the wheel of the Range Rover, or anywhere else in the truck, which meant someone was definitely guiding its systems. The question was whether or not we'd be led to an actual player in this game.

I stayed behind the truck for another two miles, lagging behind a few car lengths so I wasn't easily noticeable. I could feel Ace staring at me, and I knew it was because of the massive amount of cops that had just flown past us, headed to the scene we'd left for them. I ignored her stare, and kept my eyes locked on the Range Rover.

When it made a left at the light I followed suit, but I made the mistake of getting too close. I knew the Range Rover manufacturer had packages available for autonomous driving vehicles, and one of the features offered was evading maneuvers when your vehicle detected someone following them.

"Shit!" I growled, mashing my foot down on the gas to catch up with the now fleeing SUV.

"Bae, there's no way to follow the truck without bringing attention to ourselves. You *know* the purpose of the features assigned to evading were designed to attract the attention of the authorities," Fatz said.

I wanted to tell him to sit back and shut up, but I knew he was right. I made the right decision to give up the chase, and instead head to the location of the safe house we'd arranged. It took me an hour and a half to get to the warehouse in Alexandria, Virginia. I'd chosen such a large location because it gave us the privacy necessary for screaming, and I *fully intended* to make this nigga Gunz scream. When I pulled up alongside the truck Junior and Asad had been in, both doors opened and they hopped out.

"What took you so long, Mom? I started to come back down there for you," Junior said, pulling my driver's side door open.

"Calm down, everything is fine. Get him out of the back, and drag his ass in the building," I demanded, climbing out of the truck.

"Fatz, check the perimeter. Ace, you're with me," I said, hopping out and heading for the buildings side entrance.

The warehouse was once a furniture store, so there were odds and ends in the form of broken chairs, extra mattresses with somewhat fresh piss stains, couches without cushions. I hadn't bought it for its decor though.

"Ace, grab that chair over there and sit it in the middle of the floor so Gunz can be strapped to it. The zip ties should be in the office."

"I got you, Snow."

While she did that, I took off my shirt, which left me with just my sports bra and sweatpants on. I tied my steel-toed Timbs up tight, and then I started doing some stretches.

"Is this your new yoga studio?" Asad asked from behind me.

I turned around to the sounds of him and Junior laughing, and I gave them both of my middle fingers.

"Put him in that chair right there, funny men," I said, pointing to their destination.

The way Gunz's body flopped around limply told me he was still unconscious, but I knew how to fix that. Ace returned with the zip ties, and Gunz was secured to the chair swiftly. When they were done, I walked right up to him, raised my leg and brought my boot down on his nuts. His eyes popped open immediately, and the way his mouth opened made me think he was gonna scream, but instead he threw up. If I hadn't seen it coming, he would've gotten vomit all over my Timbs.

Even though I missed the projectile throw-up, it still made me mad he'd almost got the shit on me. I stepped forward and hit him with a vicious right-handed upper cut that rocked him backwards so fast and hard, the chair tipped over. While he was on his back, I raised my booted foot and stomped on his chest repeatedly, until his mouth was misting bright red blood into the air with every exhale of carbon dioxide from his lungs.

"You might wanna ask him some questions before you drown him in his own blood, bae," Fatz said.

I ignored him and instead, aimed my kicks towards Gunz's face and head. Two teeth scattered across the dingy floor, but it wasn't until I heard the familiar crushing of bone that I felt myself smile.

"Claudette," Fatz said more forcefully.

I stopped long enough to turn and look at him. I was about to cuss him out for interrupting me, but the look on Asad and

Junior's faces made me pause. I'd never seen the look of horrified fascination that was mirrored on their features, but I understood this was the first time they'd ever seen me in my element.

I quickly checked my thirst for blood and got back to the logical side of what we were doing here. I sat Gunz's chair up, pulled my gun out, and pressed it to his temple.

"There are things you love in this world, and if you don't tell me what I wanna know, I'm gonna find those things and erase them from existence. I promise you that. Now, does your connect know I'm alive?" I asked.

"Y-yes, and she's gonna kill you," he slurred, chuckling.

"Not if I kill her first. Where is she?" I asked.

"F-fuck you, Snow."

"Your dick ain't big enough," I replied, pulling the trigger and blowing his brains out.

"Damn," Ace murmured.

I looked to Fatz, and the understanding was clear for both of us.

"What's our next move, Mom?" Junior asked.

"And who is after us?" Asad chimed in.

My eyes stayed on Fatz, but for a different reason now and I could see he was as fucked up as I was, by Asad asking that question. The answer would devastate him...and that was why he could never find out the truth.

Aryanna

CHAPTER 10

Three Days Later

Colorado

"What did I do *wrong* though?"

"Asad, please listen to me, son. You haven't done *anything* wrong. You handled yourself well when we made that move at the basketball court, but I need you here to protect Alexia," I explained patiently.

"Why can't you hire people to guard her or have Junior stay, since it's his wife and child that need protection?"

"First of all, I can't trust hired help with the future of our family line, but I *know* I can trust you. Secondly, I need Junior with me for a reason I'm not about to explain, so you're just gonna have to trust me. We won't be gone long," I assured him.

"Yeah, and that's the same shit my birth mother told me before she disappeared."

I opened my mouth to say something to try and soothe him, but there was no lie big enough to cover the bigger one I was now running from. Instead, all I could do was pull him into my arms and hold his head against my chest.

"I know you're afraid of losing me, baby boy, but I ain't going nowhere anytime soon. I promise."

"Don't make that promise unless you can keep it," he mumbled into my chest.

I pulled back so I could look down into his brown eyes.

"I'm strong-willed, Asad, but I know I'm not bulletproof. So, I promise to do *everything* in my power to come back to you."

My words didn't erase the pain or fear from his eyes, but I could see he was giving me the benefit of the doubt for now. He hugged me tightly before letting go and heading back inside the house. I took a deep breath, hoping the crisp mountain air would somehow wash away the nightmare I was living in.

It seemed like every time I looked in Asad's face, I always had the same wish in my mind that I'd killed Phillisa when I had the fucking chance to. She'd never deserved to have Zion's son anyway and now here she was, about to possibly fuck up his life some more. I'd never be confused or mistaken for the perfect mother, but I knew I was better at it than she was. Now was the time I'd have to prove those words though, because I had to somehow save my family from losing me *and* finding out the truth.

"I thought I might find you out here," Fatz said, coming out of the house behind me.

"Yeah, I just finished talking to Asad."

"Based on the pout riding his face, I'd say that conversation didn't go too smoothly," he said, placing both of his hands on my shoulders and massaging lightly.

"Asad might have adult tendencies, but this whole situation also brings out that scared little boy I'd first met. I'm scared I'm gonna disappoint him, or worse than that, lose him."

"Snow, you're not gonna lose him. He loves you with all of his heart."

"I know that, but I also know what the truth will do to him," I replied softly.

The silence that came from Fatz following that statement told me he also understood the effect the truth would have on our lives. There weren't enough hollow platitudes in the world to make that truth feel better to swallow, which only left one option. Keep the truth buried in the darkness.

"So, do you know how you wanna handle this situation once we get back on the East Coast?"

"Yeah, but I don't think you're gonna like it," I replied, turning around to face him.

"Oh, Lord."

"Come on, let's take a ride so we can talk without the kids overhearing," I said, taking his hand and leading him down the steps.

Once we were in the truck, I drove us a couple miles away from the house to a beautiful mountain overlook.

"I've never seen snow this white," I said, taking in the view.

"It's an untouched part of the world, more or less, which keeps it pristine. I love it here."

"Me too. If we can ever get out of the game completely, then I'd wanna make this our new home. Would you be cool with that?" I asked.

"Anywhere in the world you are, I'd be cool with being there with you. Even in the grave."

His words pulled my eyes away from the tranquil snowcapped mountains so I could stare at him. I didn't have to ask if he meant what he said, because I knew he only spoke the truth with regards to his emotions. I was simply wondering if he understood how his words made me feel.

"You know I love you, right?" I asked.

"Of course, baby."

I took his hand and nodded my head because I was suddenly choked by the tears in my throat. I didn't wanna cry, I'd done enough of that to last me a few lifetimes. Right now, all I wanted was to give this good man the same love he was giving me. I slid my seat all the way back while unbuttoning my jeans.

"Wh-what are you doing?" he asked.

I didn't bother answering, I simply slid my jeans down over my hips and pulled my feet free. Before he could ask another question, I was in his lap with my lips on his, enticing his cooperation. I knew Fatz was a man of action, but I was still surprised by how swiftly he got his dick out, pulled my panties to the side and pushed up inside me. I wasn't mad though, I was turned the fuck on.

Normally, I would've taken my time to let the heat build between us, but this time I just started bouncing straight up and down on the dick like it was spring-loaded. My pussy was always tight enough to have him fighting for air, but I could feel his heart beat harder with every attack he made against my pussy walls. His hands went to my shoulders, and he pulled me down while thrusting harder upwards. I could feel the throbbing of his dick in my ribs, and that only motivated me to take more as fast as I could.

"Oh b-baby," I moaned, holding on tighter.

He grabbed a handful of my hair and used it as his anchor while he kept steadily fucking me. The rumbling inside my body felt like I was on the verge of causing an avalanche, and there was no stopping it.

"Andrew!" I screamed, as my body rocked with the force of my orgasm.

To stop from screaming more, I sunk my teeth into his shoulder and bit, until the taste of his blood oozed down my throat. He bucked hard enough to push me through the windshield, but I held on tightly and rode his ass like a wild bull. I was taking all the punishment he was delivering, but he surprised the hell out of me when he flipped me beneath him.

His passion had him ramming his dick inside me hard enough to make me feel every spring in the seat at my back. I somehow managed to pull the lever to let the seat recline backwards, but that only served to give him more room to punish me. I felt my feet hit the roof before I realized what that signified, and the next thing I knew it felt like his dick was gonna come up from my pussy, and out through my nose. I couldn't scream, I couldn't run, I couldn't even fuck him back! All I could do was whimper as he pushed my climactic aftershocks into another full-fledged orgasm of hurricane magnitude.

When I came this time, I bit my tongue hard enough to taste my own blood, but I didn't give a fuck. My pussy gushed all over his dick, and it sounded like a wet sponge being squeezed every time he dove inside me. I felt like I would lose consciousness any minute, which would've been fine by me, but before that could happen, I felt his cum rocket inside me. He kept fucking me, as his dick dumped all it had saved up for moments like this. When he finally pulled out of me, and slumped into the driver's seat I was able to put my legs down and breathe.

"G-goddammit! Are y-you mad at me?" I asked, fighting for oxygen.

"Nah, bae, I just love you like that."

I chuckled and shook my head, while reaching out for his hand. When our fingers locked, I used his strength to pull myself into a sitting position.

"We better get back," I said.

"I'll drive," he replied, passing me my jeans off of the driver's side floor.

I managed to get them back on and erase the freshly fucked look off my face by the time we pulled up at the house.

"You never did tell me what the plan is, sweetheart."

"Sorry. I got a little distracted," I said sheepishly.

He laughed as he climbed out of the truck. I followed his lead and met him at the front of the truck, where he took my hand in his. Before we could make it up on the porch, the front door opened and Ace came out, followed by Junior.

"They look serious," I said, under my breath.

"Uh-huh."

"Mom, we need to talk," Junior said immediately.

"Ok, what's up?"

"Asad is about to get his ass whooped if he keeps coming at me, about me being unable to take care of my wife and kid."

"Junior, calm down, he's just mad because I'm making him stay here and protect Alexia," I replied.

"Why? I can handle it, Mom, and you—"

"Because I said so, Junior, and I need you *not* to question me on this," I stated forcefully.

He wanted to argue, but he shut his mouth and screwed his face up instead.

"Uh, not to interrupt your little family situation, but is there a plan of action yet?" Ace asked.

"Yeah, there's a plan. We're heading back east, and I'm gonna take back what's mine," I replied.

"You're gonna what?" Fatz asked, pulling my arm until I was looking at him.

"You heard me, I'm gonna take my throne back, and that will bring her to *us.*"

"Wait, you *want* to bring the bitch who's hunting you to your front door?" Ace asked, confused.

"That's *exactly* what I'm gonna do. The reason this bitch is so effective right now, is because we're fighting blind and letting her stay in the shadows. If I step out into the open, she may *think* I'm a bigger target, but I'm actually harder to kill.

Plus, once her people see I'm alive and well, they'll push her, which could cause her to make a mistake. A fatal mistake."

"Who are her people?" Ace asked.

"The Columbians," Fatz replied, still staring at me like I had four heads with a dick in each mouth.

"Mom, that shit is *beyond* dangerous. The Columbians killed Dad, so why would you provoke them like this?"

"Because it's not what they would expect, and that's the *only way* to win this war," I replied honestly.

He stood there staring at me, looking every bit just like his daddy, and then the unthinkable happened. Before my very eyes, I watched the look in his eyes transform until I felt a chill walk across my soul, because I was staring at my late husband. The cold detachment Zion could invoke effortlessly was now possessed by our son, and it made my heart hurt.

"I'm with you, Mom, no matter what."

I nodded because I didn't trust my words at the moment.

"Are you absolutely sure about this?" Fatz asked.

I nodded again, and he gave a reluctant nod in return.

"So how are we doing this?" Ace asked.

"I'm gonna reach out to all of my old connects and let them know I'm back from the dead. Plus, I've got some new friends to make," I replied.

"The black book?" Fatz asked.

I gave him a brilliant smile, which made him pull me into his arms and kiss the top of my head.

"Do you know what they're talking about?" Ace asked.

"Nah, they've always had their own language," Junior replied.

"I'll explain everything in detail once we're on the plane, so let's get ready to move," I said, stepping back out of Fatz's arms.

We all headed into the house and two hours later, we were boarding a private jet headed to Washington D.C. I spent the first hour and a half of the flight organizing my return with the FBI, because they'd been on my ass before I vanished. Luckily for me, the *bagman* had dirt on some pretty big fish inside the bureau, but I pulled my own strings before I went that far.

Once I convinced my people I was real and *alive*, I was welcomed back with somewhat open arms. Once I told them of the dirt I had on their bosses, I was welcomed like the prodigal son returning. After that, I contacted local law enforcement, and my old law partners so they would know before the world at large. I made sure all of my legal avenues were covered, because I knew that I'd still have to answer some questions about Anastasia, and how she died. I wasn't looking forward to that, but it was unavoidable.

With all of that handled, I turned my attention to how I wanted to announce my return to the world. Social media seemed like the best way to go, but I didn't know how to do all that shit.

"Ay, Junior, I need you to help me announce my return on all the social media platforms," I said.

"*All* social media platforms?" he asked.

"Yeah."

"Alright, give me your tablet," he said, holding his hand out.

I passed it to him, and he went to work on it.

"I got a nice little social media platform myself, if you wanna stretch out a little," Ace said, pulling out her phone.

"Absolutely, the more the merrier," I said.

She nodded her head and held her phone up to take a picture of me. I quickly changed positions on the couch, fixed my dreads, and smoothed out my white silk Gucci shirt.

"Alright, go ahead," I said.

She took a few photos really quick and then she had her face in her phone doing her thing.

"I hope you know what you're doing, bae," Fatz said, sitting down next to me.

"Are you suddenly doubting me now? Like my name ain't Claudette Snow?"

"I know what your name is, and I know the reputation that comes with it. I don't doubt you in the slightest, but I have obvious concerns," he replied.

"Such as?" I asked.

"Sweetheart, you gotta remember Phillisa is *not* your only enemy. So, you popping up out of the grave is gonna cause more people than her to lick their lips. We need to be ready for that too."

I gave what he said careful consideration, and the truth in what he was saying was undeniable. I'd made *a lot* of enemies over the years, and even though I feared none of them, I was still smart enough to be aware of *all* of them.

"We've gotta lure Phillisa out...but we should be ready for whatever," I said.

He nodded his agreement and kissed me softly on the check.

"You ready, Mom?"

"As ready as I'll ever be, just tell me what I need to do."

"Look right at the camera on your tablet and say what you want the world to hear from you," he said.

I thought in silence for a moment. When I had my thoughts ready, I looked directly at the camera, and reintroduced everyone to the devil they thought they'd outrun.

Aryanna

CHAPTER 11

Carol City, Florida

One Day Later

The last place I ever thought that I'd be was back in the place where it all began, but here I was cruising the streets I'd once owned. Everything looked the same, but completely different at the same time. I had a lot of great memories here, and I tried to reflect on those as the Maybach glided through the streets.

"I didn't realize how much I missed home until now," Junior said.

His words didn't hold any anger, but the pain was undeniable, and it hit me right in my heart. My son's life had been irrevocably fucked up by circumstances and decisions beyond his control, and that shit weighed heavily on me. My inability to change the past had my vision firmly fixed on making the best future I could for those I loved. Even if I wasn't around to enjoy it with them.

"Mom, what the fuck is *that*?"

I could hear the disbelief in Junior's voice, and my eyes didn't have to follow his to know what he was looking at out the window. I'd spent an *ungodly* amount of money to rebuild Campa's mansion the way I wanted it, and I'd done it years ago. It hadn't made sense to Fatz at the time, since both of us moved with the understanding that we could *never* willingly come back to Florida. It was still a trophy to me though, and it hadn't mattered where I was at in the world, I just wanted to know this muthafucka was still standing.

The new design accommodated every need or want that anyone could have, and it was impenetrable by everything except a nuclear weapon. In essence, I'd transformed a

105

mansion into a modern castle, and now I was the dragon protecting it.

"I thought this place was destroyed years ago," Junior said.

"It was, but I had it rebuilt from the ground up, and now it's virtually indestructible. This may literally be the safest place on earth."

"That sounds good, but something had to knock this place down before, if you had to redo it. What's to stop that same thing from happening again?" Ace asked.

"Modern technology, and endless favors," I replied simply, as the car came to a stop in the driveway.

"What do you mean?" Ace asked curiously.

I smiled and waited for the driver to open my door. When I stepped out into the bright morning sunlight, I did so with eyes moving at bullet speed to take in my new surroundings and any possible threats. I detected nothing, but that only relaxed my nerves slightly. I waited for everyone to get out of the car and get a better look at the house before I fully explained.

"Ace, you weren't with us in Dubai, but my penthouse door had a translucent covering that was created by NASA. It's bulletproof, bomb-proof, but obviously not foolproof, unless it's used the right way. The house you see before you has been fortified with that same material, and the caves that run beneath the house have been lined with it as well," I said.

"Damn, are you a queen pin, or the female version of 007?" she asked, chuckling.

"Both," Fatz replied, taking my hand and squeezing it reassuringly.

"Mom, why didn't you just send Asad and Alexia here?"

"Because that would've put them on the front line of this war, and no matter how many safety precautions I've taken, you're proof that anything can happen. I won't risk their lives like that."

Junior nodded in understanding and didn't argue any further.

"Let's get settled in," Fatz said, leading the way up the front steps.

I hadn't had a chance to set the retina scanners yet since this was my first time back, so I entered the thirty-digit number sequence that deactivated all the alarms on the grounds. I ushered everyone inside and then I rearmed the three different security systems that worked in sync with one another.

"We're locked in right now, so *no one* opens a door to go outside," I announced.

"We'll wait for you in the living room, baby, go do your thing," Fatz said.

I winked at him, before heading down the hallway away from them, towards my office. I'd given the interior designer free reign when it came to decorating the fourteen bedroom, thirty thousand square foot monster of a house, but the office and its furniture had been my design. I walked in to find the cherry wood and marble desk sitting centered in the back of the office.

There were matching leather burgundy swivel chairs in front of the desk, and a huge high backed leather chair of the same color material behind the desk. To my left, there was a burgundy couch, and a glass coffee table that sat directly across from a priceless original *Mathias* oil painting. There was a bookshelf to the left of my desk, and to the right there was a huge door for a safe. Behind that door was the elevator that would take you down to the underground caves, and eventually to the escape boat that was waiting.

I knew Phillisa knew about this escape plan, because she'd used it to outrun me. The only difference now was there were machine guns positioned to shoot at anything approaching from that direction. I slipped off my six-inch Gucci heels, and let my feet sink into the Persian rug that went wall to wall throughout the room. I went straight to my desk, tapped a few buttons on my laptop, and logged into my security systems.

It took me an hour to run through all the questions, and have the system recognize me. When that was completed, I had the system run an identity diagnostic on everyone in the house or on the grounds, and then I manually went through and approved everyone except for my driver. I didn't know him to trust him, so he would always need permission to come on my property.

After all the security precautions were momentarily addressed, I started in on my phone calls. I ordered everything I could think of we would need to survive in this house without venturing out, including weapons of mass destruction. I didn't find those on Amazon, but I managed to round up a lot of what was needed. A knock on the door broke my concentration, but I swallowed my attitude when I saw Junior standing in the doorway holding a sandwich.

"Fatz said you need to eat this, even if I gotta force it down your throat."

"Did you ask him why he's trying to get you killed?" I asked, laughing.

"I'd die for you and your wellbeing, Mom."

His statement froze my laughter in my throat, especially because I knew he meant every word he'd spoken. He walked over and put the sandwich in front of me, and then he took a seat in the chair across from me.

"Are you really gonna watch me eat this, Junior?"

"That depends."

"On what?" I asked.

"I'll treat you like an adult if you treat me like one."

"And what's that supposed to mean, son?"

"Why did you bring me here, instead of letting me stay with Alexia?"

Part of me had anticipated this question, but I'd honestly been looking for it to come sooner. Now that he'd actually asked it though, I wasn't quite sure where to begin. The only thing I knew for sure, was that I wasn't about to damage my relationship with him by lying.

"I needed you by my side, because I had to keep Asad away from the person who's after us," I replied.

"Who's after us, and why is Asad the one you're protecting the most?"

Despite the nonchalant tone of voice he'd used, I could still hear that it was upsetting him that I was moving like Asad was somehow my favorite kid.

"I had to keep him out of the way, because it's his mother that got you shot in Dubai. It's her that's after me," I admitted.

"But I thought his mom was dead..."

"It's so much more than complicated, Junior. When I'd first kidnapped Asad it had been to force her to come to me. I was hurt by the fact that she'd had a baby by your dad, but even more than that, I was enraged by how she'd played me. When Asad got shot everything changed, and all I knew was I had to protect Zion's son. Some people may have called me stupid had they known what my internal struggle was, but I didn't care because right was right. I've never regretted my decision to raise Asad as my own, away from the malicious intentions of Phillisa. My only regret is that I didn't kill her ass when I had the chance."

"So, does she know you've raised Asad, or that he's still alive?"

"Honestly, Junior, I don't know what that bitch knows, and that's part of the reason I needed to entice her to come out in the open."

He sat back in the chair, rubbing his chin and thinking hard enough for me to smell wood burning. I had no idea what was running through his mind, or which way he was attacking the information I'd given him, but I knew to give him time. I picked up my sandwich and started eating it while responding to emails on my computer.

"So, what's your endgame, Mom?"

I looked up from the monitor and finished chewing before opening my mouth to respond.

"Kill her without Asad knowing anything, and then getting back to our lives," I replied.

"Is that realistic?"

"What do you mean?" I asked, putting the sandwich down.

"I mean, I was watching you with dude who tried to have you and Fatz killed. I've never got to see you in your element, but now that I have, I feel like I know the *real* you. You're Claudette Snow, and that's more than being a mom, or my dad's widow. You're a force of nature, Mom, and you can't go back to hiding from that just to keep us safe. You have to let us live our lives with your guidance, not your shielding."

I wanted to argue with him like he was still that nine-year-old boy who had a crush on the girl next door, but he wasn't. He was a man and a soon-to-be father, which meant he had a right to give me his opinion.

"I can't keep putting my family in danger, Junior, so I can't be who I used to be."

"You say it like it's your day job, or some Halloween costume. You *are* Claudette Snow! That means you can only keep your family safe by being who you were born to be. The reason you feel like you're at a disadvantage right now, or like this bitch caught you off guard, is because you weren't being who you *really* are. Mom, I remember the security you kept around me. I'll never forget my godfather, Tony, and how you two would move the world for me and your people. You're not some suburban housewife, or some soccer mom handling the carpool. You're a goddamn *boss,* so you gotta move like one. You damn sure raised us with that mentality! When this is over, and we come out on top, you have to make sure we stay there."

The passion in his voice brought tears to my eyes and made my heartbeat faster. His tone, and the look in his eyes was the *exact* same look Zion would give me when he was spitting straight facts at me. The flipping I felt in my stomach wasn't a new feeling, but it did reaffirm what I'd been contemplating. Now that I was back to reclaim my throne, I wouldn't give it up to nothing and no one.

"I hear what you're saying, son, and I appreciate you. I'm gonna do what I gotta do."

"Good. Now finish that sandwich before I tell Fatz," he said, smiling as he got up.

I scanned my desk quickly for something to throw at him, but I didn't find anything before he was gone from my sight. When I picked up my sandwich, I could feel the smile on my face, and it felt good to experience this simple action of contentment. I'd just put the last bite of food in my mouth when my phone started buzzing in my pocket. I pulled it out to see an incoming FaceTime call from my lawyer.

"Good morning, Kelsey, what's up?"

"I wanted to let you know I met with the assistant district attorney about the murder of Anastasia Morano and there's nothing linking you to that. The house wasn't registered in your name, it was registered in hers, and because it was brand new there weren't any new cameras installed. The standard ones that come with the property happened to malfunction on that day."

"Well, I guess that's good news then," I said.

"It is, but the rest of what I'm about to say may not be. I had all the deeds to the properties you own updated so that there wouldn't be any questions about their validity. The paper trail for all of your shell companies is ironclad, so your ownership from that angle is above reproach. However, there's been a claim made against the land your fortress in Carol City sits on."

"What kind of claim? I bought this property once it was seized by the feds," I replied.

"The claim was made by the deceased owner's daughter and she's claiming the sale was illegal because the property wasn't publicly offered before you bought it. The claim has been tied up in court for years, because it's so hard to get through your shell companies to determine individual ownership. Now that you've resurfaced, I suggest we get this settled. *Especially* if you're making that your primary residence."

My initial reaction to hearing this was complete and utter anger, but then the wheels in my mind started spinning rapidly. Campa only had one child, and I knew that because I'd had that angle thoroughly investigated, once Phillisa had come out of nowhere. So, the only one who could've made a claim against the property was her.

"Kelsey, I need you to find any information you can on the person who made the claim, so I can make them an offer to back off."

"I'll get back to you," she replied, hanging up.

I sat my phone on the desk, while considering all of the ways I could play this angle. The information on Phillisa could be extremely old, but there would be some clue as to how to get in touch with her right now. *That* was the smoking gun, and I fully intended to use it.

"Alexa, intercom on. Summon Fatz to my office," I demanded.

A few seconds later I heard the speaker come on in the living room, and a computerized voice relayed my message to Fatz. By the time he got to my office I'd come up with a simple, yet effective, way of going about things.

"What's good, baby?"

"I might have a lead on tracking Phillisa down," I said.

"Where is she?"

"I don't know, but as soon as I find out, we're gonna burn the world around her until she's kneeling before us," I replied.

Aryanna

CHAPTER 12

Atlanta, Georgia

Seventy-two Hours Later

"Are you sure this is where she's gonna be?" Fatz asked, looking out of the side window.

"That's what my intel said, but..."

I was looking at the kids filing out of the building, wondering what the hell Phillisa could possibly be doing at a school.

"Do you think she's a teacher?" Junior asked, from the backseat.

"Hell no!" I said emphatically, shaking my head.

"Well, there has to be *some* type of explanation as to why your people think she's here," Ace said.

I'd kept track of Phillisa for a while and there was never any mention of her having another kid, so I doubted we were here because of her being on the PTA. If I knew her, there was some type of angle being played.

"So, do we wait, or nah?" Fatz asked, looking over at me.

This was the second day that we'd showed up here expecting to catch sight of Phillisa without anything to show for it.

"Nah, let's go back to the club and regroup," I said.

Fatz started the truck, but his hand froze in midair when he went to put it in gear.

"What's wrong?" I asked.

"There's a motorcade coming up right now," Fatz replied.

Seconds later, a line of five identical, dark blue 2033 Chevy Suburbans pulled up in front of the school and stopped. We were approximately ten feet away behind the mirror tint, but my eyes were wide open and looking hard. It seemed like five full minutes before anyone got out of the truck, and when there was movement, it came in the form of all the doors opening at once.

"She doesn't travel light, does she?" Ace asked rhetorically.

I didn't say shit, I just kept staring until the unimaginable became my reality, and Phillisa appeared from out of the third truck. Her once long hair was now cut in a short bob, but that was the only difference that stuck out to me. Her body was still tight, and this was easy to see, even with the green and tan thigh-high trench coat she was wearing.

"What do you wanna do, bae?" Fatz asked.

"With all of them niggas out there, what option is there besides regrouping and coming at her a different way?" Ace asked.

I didn't answer her question, I just kept my eyes locked on Phillisa as she disappeared inside the private Catholic school. If she always travelled this heavy, then there was never gonna be an opportune time to run down on her. Right now might be the best and worst time though, because with all these kids out here, Phillisa and her goons might be hesitant to engage in a gunfight. A moment's hesitation changed a fight, no matter how much of an underdog one was.

"Mom, what's the play?"

I didn't have to look at him to know the expression riding his features, but I was still hesitant.

"There's bound to be *a lot* of surveillance here, Snow, given how popular school shootings are," Fatz said.

When I looked over at him, I could tell he'd used my silence to read my mind, but I wasn't upset.

"The opportunities will be few and far between," I replied.

"Understood, but I don't know if you even have enough leverage to get out of that box once you open it," Fatz said.

"Are you *really* thinking about engaging with her right here, right now?" Ace asked with obvious disbelief in her voice.

I ignored her question, along with the sounds of Junior's soft laughter. I had no idea what he found funny, but knowing him, he was just getting a kick out of the thought of his mom snapping the fuck out. The risk was immense, but the reward was just as great, and that's where my mind kept getting stuck. When I caught sight of the front door to the school opening and Phillisa's entourage reemerging, I knew the time for deep contemplation was over.

"Fatz, lock this street down," I ordered.

He immediately started tapping on his phone, while I quickly checked my twin automatic Beretta 9mm pistols, equipped with two fifty-round drums.

"This is insane," Ace said, under her breath.

I started to say some slick shit, but this was one of the reasons why Fatz and I had swiftly put together a team of hittas on our second day back.

"They're ready," Fatz said.

The flow of traffic, as it pertained to children, was getting thinner, but there were still handfuls of kids stumbling out into the bright afternoon sunlight. Phillisa was moving with the flow like she didn't have a care in the world, but my focus was on the boy who was about eight feet behind her, surrounded by her men. I couldn't get a good look at him, but it was obvious the guards were there for him, which meant he was important to her.

"Aim for the kid with the guards," I said.

"A-aim for the kid?" Ace asked, in disbelief.

"Yep. Shoot to wound when it comes to the boy, but knock the tops off of everyone else," I replied, putting one gun in my lap, while opening my door slowly.

"Snow, are you sure—"

"Don't bitch up now, Ace," Junior said, popping the clip out of his Ruger-57, before slamming it back in and chambering a round.

I didn't need to ask if everyone was ready, and that allowed me to keep my focus on what was in front of me. When I stepped out of the truck, my team moved with me the same way Phillisa's had, and within seconds everyone realized we were in a Mexican standoff.

She stared at me for a few seconds before recognition hit her squarely in the mouth. I couldn't see her eyes behind her Black Billionaire frames, but the heat coming from her was unmistakable. The boy was suddenly concealed from view, and several hands slid not-so-inconspicuously inside their suit jackets.

The smirk on Phillisa's face reminded me instantly of why I hated her with everything in me, but it also reminded me of why she could never be me. She hesitated, but I was 'bout this life. I raised both pistols in her direction and held the triggers down until the bass boomed like I had my bullets hooked up to the school's loudspeakers. Before the first bullet found its mark, the screams started, and kids were scrambling faster than any drill I'd seen run for these scenarios. I wasn't worried about hitting anyone or anything except for Phillisa, and that's the direction I kept my guns trained.

The active shooter siren screamed through the air like the tornado warnings of old, signaling to me that we were now on a clock as far as response time. I stepped from behind the safety of the truck's door and advanced on Phillisa while pumping bullets at her goons. The two men closest to her lost their mustaches simultaneously and dropped at her feet. I adjusted my aim to shoot where she would be in a few seconds, because she took off running, but she made a quick grab for a child that made me pause before firing. I tried to adjust my aim again and the angle I was shooting from, but before I could do that, she'd made it to the safety of one of her trucks.

"*Grenade launcher!*" I yelled, pointing towards Phillisa's location.

My men immediately switched their focus, but by the time the first grenade sailed in that direction, I could hear the roar of a diesel engine beneath her hood. Even if I hadn't ordered my team to box her and her people in, she still wouldn't have been able to drive out of here. The street surrounding her trucks opened up after several grenades rained down on it, and Atlanta experienced an historical landslide. As trucks slid down into a newly created sinkhole the sounds of car alarms sounding off added to the overall feel of panic swirling around us.

There were both parents and teachers running around like this was the apocalypse the Bible had warned about. It would've been comical had I not been stalking my prey, weaving through the stationary vehicles towards Phillisa. Just as I reached the back bumper of the truck, she hit the gas pedal and drove straight up on the grass. There was no way out for her, but she made a pretty target for us to hit up.

I could see the paint peeling from where the high velocity hollow point rounds were knocking chunks out of the re enforced metal in the truck, but it wasn't slowing her forward progress down. I took aim at the windows, but my bullets bounced off of them just like they did the truck's armor. Me and my team were chasing the truck on foot because there was literally nowhere to go, but Phillisa did the unthinkable. She stopped long enough to scoop up what was left of her bodyguards and the little boy with them, and then she drove her truck straight up the school's steps, through the front door.

The sound of wood splintering was barely audible over the growl of the truck's engine. My feet were rooted to the ground in shock, and by the time I could move again, all I saw in front of me was a cloud of thick black smoke.

"We gotta go, bae," Fatz said, grabbing me by the arm.

I followed his lead at a dead run back to my truck, where Junior was behind the wheel already.

"Hang on," he said, once I'd slid into the passenger seat.

I thought he was about to try and navigate around the hole in the earth, and the vehicles burning in front of us, but instead he drove right up on the grass like Phillisa had.

"What are you *doing,* boy?" I asked, holding on to the armrest.

"That bitch don't get away," Junior growled through clenched teeth.

With the way he was driving, and the determination covering his face, I knew that there wasn't any room for argument. We roared through the schoolhouse, using the path of destruction Phillisa had created. For a second, I thought we wouldn't make it through because my truck wasn't as jacked up as hers, but we came out into a grass covered playground and I caught sight of her smoke cloud a few blocks away.

"There!" I screamed, pointing towards the blue suburban that was fleeing.

Junior wasted no time pointing us in her direction and stomping on the gas pedal. Her diesel engine may have sounded angrier and given her more torque, but we had speed on our side. It took less than a minute for Junior to have us riding that bitch's bumper, and I immediately leaned out the window with my gun. I took aim at the tires this time and tried to shred them with rapid gunfire. I hit the left rear tire first, before switching my attention to the right side. By the time I saw the right rear tire go flat, the left rear was back at standard height and rolling smoothly.

"The goddamn tires are bullet resistant!" I yelled in frustration, leaning back inside the truck.

"Ram their ass!" Ace suggested.

When I looked back to ask her what the point was, she was already leaning out the window, with the grenade launcher clutched in her grip.

"You gotta time it perfectly, son, because I'm bettin' she has magnetic suspension to keep the truck grounded, and bomb proof plates under the truck. If you tap her into a quick spin when Ace hits her with the grenade, the explosion should be enough to knock the truck over. Ace, make sure you use the adhesive grenades," I said.

He nodded, and I could see him gripping the steering wheel tighter in concentration.

"She's going for the highway, so hit her before she gets on the ramp," I demanded.

"I'm ready!" Ace hollered, before leaning out the window.

When I looked back to Junior, I expected to see his nerves written all over his face, but there wasn't a bead of sweat in sight. He dropped the truck into overdrive and hit the gas so he picked up speed. When Phillisa tried to merge onto the off-ramp, Junior swung the steering wheel to the right hard enough to send us into the rear quarter panel of her SUV. As soon as we made contact Ace fired two grenades.

One went under the truck and out of view, while the other one stuck to the running board under the rear driver side door. They blew within seconds of each other and pushed the heavy Chevy Suburban up and over onto its side. Junior hit the brakes, and we watched as the truck slid to a stop up against the guardrail. Junior put the truck in park and opened the door to hop out, but I put a hand on his arm.

"That truck is as secured as an armored vehicle full of bank money. You getting out just makes you an easier target. Let me see how far away our people are," I said, reaching for my phone.

"I got it, bae," Fatz said, from the backseat next to Ace.

While he did that, I kept my eyes on the truck in front of me, contemplating my approach. The sudden opening of one of the back doors scrambled my thoughts but the appearance of a little boy's head brought me right back into the reality of the moment.

"Watch my back," I said, opening my door quickly.

By the time I stepped out and made it around to the front of the truck, a guard and Phillisa had made it out of the truck too. By now there were cars pulling over along the side of the road and good Samaritans were getting out to assist. A crowd only worked to her advantage, but I didn't know how to disperse them without attracting more unwanted attention.

The only thing I could think to do was smoke the bitch and get out of Dodge immediately. I raised my pistol and aimed at Phillisa, but I caught sight of the little boy, and suddenly my arm was back at my side.

"It *can't be*," I whispered in disbelief.

My brain was processing the impossible information as fast as it could, but it still felt like I was thinking under water. I felt a presence to my left, and I turned in anticipation of finding Fatz, but it was someone else.

"Junior, wait," I said, reaching for his arm.

I didn't move fast enough to stop the first shot from flying, but he didn't fire another one. When I turned to look back at Phillisa, she was laying on the side of the SUV, and the little boy was under her.

CHAPTER 13

"Mom, we gotta go...We gotta *go!*" he said insistently, grabbing my arm and pulling me towards the truck.

My hesitation was wrapped up in my disbelief at what I'd seen, but the sound of approaching sirens penetrated the fog enough for me to move my feet. I turned and ran back to my truck and hopped in the passenger seat. As Junior pulled off, I put my head down in between my legs, let my guns drop to the floor, and struggled to breathe. All the noise swirling around me only added to the weight on my chest, and it was a valiant fight to keep the vomit down.

"You ok, bae?" Fatz asked, rubbing my back.

I couldn't speak because all I kept seeing was the little boy lying beneath Phillisa.

"Did she get shot?" Ace asked.

"Nah, she's fine," Fatz said.

Junior took a corner fast, tilting the truck until we were riding on two wheels.

"Slow down," I growled, clenching my stomach muscles tightly.

He got the truck back on four wheels, but his speed didn't decrease in the slightest. I wanted to scream at him to slow this muthafucka *down*, but I needed to get away from everything that had just happened. I'd anticipated a lot of things when I'd organized my thoughts around attacking Phillisa, but there had been *no way* to prepare for what I'd seen today.

The streets were the jungle, and survival was built off of anticipation of your opponent's moves. You had to be able to see what was coming in order to know what to do next, and when you didn't know what was coming you ran the risk of being caught off guard. Phillisa hadn't caught me off guard, the bitch had caught me completely flatfooted.

"Where are we going?" Junior asked.

My first thought was to tell him to get the fuck out of Florida immediately, but what came out of my mouth was the polar opposite.

"Go back."

"*What*?" Junior and Fatz yelled in unison.

"*Go back!*" I stated forcefully, looking at Junior first and then Fatz.

"Am I missing something?" Ace asked, with a bewildered expression on her face.

"If so, then we *all are*," Fatz said, staring at me like he was watching my brain leak out of my nose.

"Mom, you can't be serious. We can't go—"

"Make me repeat myself again, Junior, I fucking *dare you*," I growled through clenched teeth, whirling on him.

My son knew me well enough to be fearful of me, but his hesitation was still obvious. On the one hand, I understood it because it *sounded* crazy, but he knew who his mother was and what I was about. The trust I'd earned when it came to him was immeasurable.

"Baby, what the hell is going on?"

"Fatz we *have* to go back, and you just have to trust me," I replied, giving him a look I knew was hard to interpret.

"I do trust you, Snow..."

The *but* he wanted to interject was ringing loudly throughout the truck, despite the fact that he hadn't spoken it out loud.

"Junior," I said, looking at him again.

"I'm going back, Mom."

His words matched his actions when he swung a U-turn in the middle of the road and pushed the gas pedal to the floor.

"I'm so lost, but fuck it," Ace said, as she reloaded her gun.

Fatz followed her lead, and I did the same for me and Junior. By the time we pulled up on the scene, we were ready for round two.

"Damn, the cops got here fast as fuck," Fatz said.

"Pull over a few feet back from the last cop car," I instructed.

When Junior finally brought the truck to a stop, I could feel all eyes land on me, awaiting my next move. The risk behind just sitting here was enough to have me questioning my own damn sanity, but in my heart, I knew I was only doing what I had to do.

"Everybody sit tight, I'll be right back," I said, opening my door and stepping out before anyone could speak.

When I'd reloaded my gun, I'd switched my custom magazines out for the standard one my gun came with, so that I could conceal my weapon. I tucked the pistol down in the front of my jeans, pulled my shirt over it, and closed the truck door. I pulled my phone out to give the appearance of a nosy bystander as I walked towards Phillisa's overturned SUV.

The cop cars had been blocking my vision of the scene, so I was surprised to see both bodies had been moved from where I'd left them once I got to the bumper of the last cop car. That surprise quickly morphed into shock when I saw the paramedics working on the little boy in the back of the ambulance, and Phillisa sitting on the bumper of the ambulance giving her statement to a cop. There were three other cops evaluating the crash, and securing the perimeter, and amazingly no one was paying attention to me.

The guard that had been with Phillisa was laid out on the ground next to their truck, obviously dead, which meant the only thing standing between me and her were the cops. I don't know if she sensed me, but she suddenly looked up and locked eyes with me. I'd never seen fear in Phillisa until right now, and it was fleeting. She glanced around briefly before looking back at me, and smirking. I knew she felt ten feet tall and bulletproof right now, which was just another mistake to add to the many she'd made.

The ways to handle this situation rolled through my mind, but when I heard the paramedics holler that the boy was stable, and they needed to go, I reacted with complete disregard for the consequences that were sure to come next. I pulled my gun out and enjoyed the look of fear return to Phillisa's. I aimed at her for a split second, and then I shifted slightly up and to the left of her head.

"No!" she screamed, hopping to her feet faster than the paramedics probably gave her credit for.

She wasn't faster than a speeding bullet though. I hit the paramedic with a headshot that made him fold up into the medicine cabinets, and I pumped three bullets into the boy on the stretcher. I had to trust my aim was good, because my attention swung to the cops that were moving around the scene. The gunshots had gotten their attention of course, and that made me swing my gun in their direction while continuing to let shots off.

One cop dropped, and the other two took cover, which allowed me to back up. I was almost back behind the first cop car, when I got knocked sideways by the bullet that punched me in my stomach. I shot my arm out in anticipation of hitting the ground, but I found myself being caught before I fell.

"I gotchu," Ace said, pulling me out of the line of fire.

I heard more shots and guns going off behind us somewhere, but my focus was on the pain I was feeling, because *this shit* had some bite to it.

"G-get me back to the truck," I panted, making sure not to drop my gun or my phone, as I turned and put my arm around her shoulders.

"I got you, come on."

As we moved towards my truck, I caught sight of Junior and Fatz shooting and the guilt I felt hit me like a sledgehammer.

"We gotta g-go," I said loudly.

The look of pure anger that Fatz turned on me made me shut the fuck up and move as fast as I could back to my truck. Ace helped me up onto the backseat and then she jumped behind the wheel. When she hit the horn twice, Junior and Fatz suddenly appeared and hopped in.

"Go!" Fatz demanded, while he and Junior leaned out the window and kept shooting.

We made it away without any more damage being done, but it seemed like every second that passed brought more intense pain from my stomach. I felt like I wanted to throw up, but if I did it would probably be my life coming out of my mouth.

"How bad is it?" Fatz asked, pulling up my shirt so that he could take a look.

"Hurts like hell," I grunted.

"Mom, why the *fuck* did you make us go back? And then you start a fucking shootout *by yourself*! *Are you trying to get killed*?" Junior screamed, shaking with fury as he turned to look at me.

I could tell he was only getting madder because he was scared of losing me, and I understood that fear all too well.

"My-my instincts told me to make sure it-it was done," I replied honestly.

"You didn't have to *start fucking shooting*!" Junior raged.

"I know you're mad, but I need you to calm down, Junior, and keep your eyes open," Fatz said, while he ripped my shirt and used it to wipe the wound.

"I'm calm...but that shit doesn't make *no* sense, Fatz, and you *know* it doesn't. Mom is smarter than that."

The look Fatz was giving me spoke loudly of how much he agreed with Junior, but he kept his mouth shut and his hands busy.

"*Ahhhh, shit!*" I screamed when he started applying pressure.

"The bullet is definitely still in there, and we gotta get it out if we're gonna stop the bleeding," Fatz said.

"Do you want me to go to the hospital?" Ace asked.

"Not gonna happen, especially not with her infamous ass face being freshly imprinted on the general public's brain," Junior replied.

"I kn-know a guy," I said.

"Are you talking about the same guy who stitched me up?" Fatz asked.

"Y-yeah, Kevin is his name. He has his own practice now."

I laid my gun on the seat beside me and focused on my phone in my other hand. I'd reached out to Kevin to let him know I was back in town, but I hadn't seen him yet. He'd taken my resurrection better than anyone, because he'd known I wasn't dead, but he also knew that if I was back, I was bringing hell with me. I sent him a text now, telling him I needed him ASAP and I gave him instructions on where to meet me.

"Go back to the-the house," I said.

"I'll make the preparations to leave Florida and the country once we have Alexia and Asad," Junior said.

"J-just make the arrangements for you all," I said.

"Snow you can't *seriously* be thinking about staying here now. Fuck the fact that we missed the target, and focus on the fact that every law enforcement agency known to man is about to get involved," Ace said.

Fatz and I shared another look because no words were necessary. The danger was unquestionable, as was my willingness to see this shit through until the end. Fatz knew that, which meant the question in his eyes wasn't about this decision I had to make.

"What's going on, bae? You're leaving me in the dark right now, and that ain't what we do."

"Fatz, you-you have to trust me—"

"It's not a question of trust, Claudette, it's about my unwillingness to be kept in the dark any further. You asked me to trust you a little while ago, and then you did some suicidal shit. I need you to explain what is going on in your mind right now."

The amount of love, trust, and understanding in his eyes brought my very raw emotions to the surface. I knew I could tell him *anything* because we'd been through everything, but still the words that I needed to form wouldn't come. Normally he wouldn't push, but I could tell by how thick the silence was that he needed answers.

"The-the boy is him," I said.

"Him who? What are you talking about mom?" Junior asked.

I ignored him and kept my attention on Fatz. At first, he didn't say anything, and the questioning look didn't fade, but suddenly the lights came on behind his eyes.

"That's impossible, Claudette. There's absolutely *no goddamn way* what you're suggesting is true," he replied.

"I'm not suggesting sh-shit, I'm *telling you* it was him," I said.

"Him who? Mom, what are you talking about?" Junior asked again.

My phone vibrating in my hands gave me a momentary distraction, but I could feel Fatz eyes on me even as I was reading.

"Hurry to the h-house, Ace," I said.

"Mom, are you gonna keep ignoring me?"

"Junior, let it go. Right now, we need to focus on getting your mother healed," Fatz said.

My hand went to his face, and I caressed it gently to show my appreciation.

"I love you," I said softly.

"I love you too, baby."

I gave him the best smile I could muster, while trying not to grimace in pain from the pressure he was applying on my wound. We made it to the house a short while later, and thankfully, Kevin was waiting on me. Fatz carried me into our bedroom and laid me on the bed so Kevin could work his magic.

"Same old Snow, huh?" Kevin asked.

"Nothing changes, Doc, if we're lucky we just get older," I replied.

"True. I'm gonna give you a shot for the pain, and then we'll get started," he said.

I nodded as he filled a syringe with a clear liquid and approached my bedside. He swiftly administered the shot a few inches away from the wound in my stomach, and almost instantly the pain became bearable. I was finally able to take a deep breath, and my body wasn't as tense as it had been.

"We gotta move quick, Doc, because we don't know when the authorities might show up," Fatz said.

"Understood. Are you ready?" I replied.

I didn't have to search for Fatz's hand because he immediately sat down and laced our fingers together. While Kevin grabbed his tools and went to work, Fatz and I had a conversation that was completely nonverbal, yet a hundred percent understandable. I knew he understood the pain that went deeper than this bullet wound. It went deeper than the past we'd been through, even me losing Zion and Tony. The truth that existed between Fatz and me in this moment was more proof that time didn't heal all wounds.

"It's gonna be ok, baby," Fatz whispered, stroking my hair gently.

I managed to give him a genuine smile before the pain medication kicked up a final notch and swept me off to the land of the unconscious. When I woke up, Fatz's hand was still snuggled firmly in my own, but instead of sitting next to me, he was lying beside me in the bed asleep. I tried to gently shift my weight so I could get up and go to the bathroom, but as soon as I moved his eyes snapped open.

"Are you ok?" he asked immediately.

"Yeah, I'm fine. I just need to pee."

"Come on, I'll help you," he offered, sliding from the bed and then scooping me up in his arms.

"You think you're slick, nigga, but you ain't getting no pussy just because you help me use the bathroom."

He chuckled and shook his head as he carried me into the bathroom and put me on my feet.

"Try not to fall in. I'm gonna get you something to drink so that you can rehydrate, and take your pills," he said, kissing me on the top of my head.

I waited until he disappeared before testing my flexibility when it came to sitting on the toilet. There was a sharp pain when I first bent over, but it quickly passed. I used the bathroom, washed my hands, and then went in search of Fatz.

I found all three of them in the living room, seemingly hypnotized by the T.V. Ace saw me first and shut the TV off immediately.

"How you feeling, Snow?" she asked.

"I'm good... what's up with y'all?" I asked, picking up on the vibe in the room.

Neither Junior nor Fatz made eye contact with me, and Ace opened her mouth, but no words came out.

"Don't everybody speak at once," I said sarcastically.

"Phillisa is still alive, but... the little boy in the back of the ambulance was pronounced dead at the scene. How did you miss her at point blank range, but manage to hit an innocent kid?" Junior asked, looking at me with clear suspicion.

When Fatz looked at me, I could tell he didn't know what to say, but I knew if I asked him, he would tell me to lay out the truth.

"Junior, I don't owe you no lies, but are you sure you want the truth?" I asked.

"Yes, Mom, I'm not a little kid anymore."

I searched his eyes for a long moment, but I didn't get the sense that he was ready for this ugliness he was asking for.

"Tell him, bae," Fatz said softly.

I took a deep breath and squared my shoulders.

"My focus was the boy first, and that's how she got spared."

"But why, Mom? I get that she needs to die, so why not deal with that first? Her son wasn't a threat, he was—"

"He wasn't her son. He was mine," I said quickly.

CHAPTER 14

I saw the wind get knocked out of Junior instantly, so there was no need to wonder if he'd heard me. If that wasn't enough though, the shock on his face said it all.

"Did you-did you just say the kid in the ambulance was *your* son?" Ace asked.

"Yeah," I replied simply.

Junior still hadn't said anything, but something had definitely changed. It started with the fact that his gun had suddenly appeared in his hand.

"What did you say?" Junior asked softly.

"I said I didn't shoot Phillisa's son, because he was my son. Technically."

"Explain, Mother," he growled softly.

"First, you need to put your gun away before I start to think the wrong thing," I said.

Hearing this made both Ace and Fatz turn to look at Junior. I could tell Fatz was ready to slap some sense into Junior, but he didn't move, because he knew I had this under control. Junior tucked his gun and crossed his arms over his chest in demonstration that he wasn't trying to be disrespectful, but he wanted answers *right* now.

"Do you remember when I'd left Colorado with everybody, but I didn't come back right away?" I asked.

"You mean the time you were missing? Don't look so surprised, Mom, I wasn't dumb then and I'm not dumb now."

"I know that, Zion, and you can drop the sarcasm before you and I have a problem," I said seriously.

I could tell by the way he clenched his jaw that he was big mad, but he kept himself under control. What he was about to hear was *definitely* gonna make him angrier, so I said a small prayer before I continued.

"Phillisa double-crossed me and handed me over to her dad. He had plans for me, but I managed to convince her to bring me back to Colorado, because that's where Asad was. The whole time they had me captive, I was drugged because that made it easier to move me around...it also made it easier to rape me."

"Whoa," Ace said softly.

The look on Junior's face changed instantly, and his anger shifted to a concern that made him step forward towards me.

"Mom," he choked out, taking me in his arms.

I'd been doing my best not to cry, but the moment my son put his arms around me, I was lost in my own tears. He held me tight, as my body rocked with a sadness I'd been unable to outrun or deal with.

I couldn't put into words all that I felt now or then, but I knew even if I could, it might not justify my actions to him. All I could do was put myself at his mercy, because as my son, he meant that much to me. I wiped my eyes, took a deep breath, and stepped back so the ugly truth could be fully laid bare.

"I'd thought I'd started my period while they had me captive, because I was bleeding, but once we were on the run, I realized I was pregnant. Fatz helped me put the pieces together. I had no idea who the father was, but the feeling in the pit of my stomach made me track down Campa's DNA and run it. Unfortunately, by the time we were able to do that, it was too late to have an abortion. So, I delivered the baby, and it was taken away before I could ever look at him or her."

"I gave the baby to a missionary church in Florida, and I did it anonymously," Fatz interjected.

"So how the fuck did your kid end up in the hands of your enemy? And why didn't she kill him or use him as leverage?" Ace asked.

"I don't know how, but my assumption is that she knew about the rape, and so she expected the pregnancy. It probably gave her a way of tracking me, but we moved so fast once I had the baby, she never got the chance to take a shot at us. As for why she didn't kill him, well that's because he's her half-brother and he probably filled the void from the child she'd lost," I replied.

"And you killed him because he never should've been born," Junior said softly, nodding his head in realization and understanding.

"I couldn't think straight knowing she was actually raising the product of my rape. I know I should be better than that, but I'm not—"

"It's ok, Mom. I get it. If something like that would've happened to Alexia, I wouldn't have been able to deal. I get it," Junior said.

"Unfortunately, the cops don't get it because they're hunting heads on this one," Ace said.

"The news report we were just watching hasn't named you, but that could only be a matter of time. Phillisa definitely knows who it was that killed the little boy everybody thinks is her son," Fatz said.

"Yeah, but would anyone actually *believe* a mother would kill her own son?" Ace asked.

We all contemplated that question quietly, but when I looked at Ace, I could tell she had something on her mind.

"What are you thinking, Ace?" I asked.

"Just that it might be smarter to get in front of this and that way you control the narrative."

"How do you mean?" I asked curiously.

"Well, you've got *a lot* of connections, so if you were to slide them a DNA sample to run against the little boy, then you cause doubt in Phillisa instantly. She has to explain how she came to have your son, a son you can tell your connections was kidnapped after birth. You look like the victim, and she looks like the villain."

The smile I turned on Ace was the most genuine I'd felt on my face in a *long damn time*. She'd literally just smashed a whole bird's nest with one stone and made omelets for breakfast. When I looked at Fatz, I saw the same look of admiration in his eyes that matched the feeling in my stomach.

"You're a fucking genius, Ace," I said.

The smile she gave me in return was part pride and part seduction, and I winked at her to let her know we'd get back to the latter.

"So, what's our next move?" Junior asked.

"I contact my lawyer first and then I go to my people," I replied.

Junior put his hands on my shoulders and looked down into my face.

"No more secrets, Mom. I love you and I trust you, but I need you to stop treating me like a little kid. Ok?"

"Yes, son, I understand."

He pulled me towards him and kissed my cheek. That shouldn't have brought the tears back that I'd just had to beat back, but in this moment, I remembered all the times his dad had done the same thing. Junior would've been too young to remember that, which proved his movements were instinctive, and more proof that his dad lived within him. I might've hated my ex-husband, but I was eternally grateful for the wonder that was my son.

"While I get to work, I want you all to prepare to go after Phillisa. This plan should bring her out into the open, and expose her vulnerabilities, especially if I can get her detained," I said.

"We got you, bae," Fatz said.

I smiled at him, and then retreated to my office. I jumped on the phone immediately and spoke to my attorney about my plans. She agreed to have two independent labs come retrieve DNA samples from me, so there wouldn't be any question of authenticity. When that was done, I contacted my people at the FBI, because I knew that kidnapping was definitely federal territory.

It didn't take me long to convince them to make a move against Phillisa and her cartel. By the time I was done with that conversation, the labs were here to get their samples from me. All of that only took around fifteen minutes, and then they were gone like they'd never been there.

"How are you holding up?" Fatz asked, coming into the office with a bag in his hand.

"If that's a spicy chicken sandwich from Popeye's, then I'm about to be *so much* better."

"You know I got you, bae," he replied, handing me the bag before sitting down across from me.

I quickly unwrapped the sandwich and took a huge bite.

"I take it your wound is healing up," he said, chuckling.

"Fuck you, and yes, it is. I should've shot that bitch, and then I wouldn't have run the risk of getting shot again."

"Don't worry, I'll stand between you and the next bullet," he replied.

I didn't have to look at him to know just how genuine his statement was, because I knew I'd do the same thing for him.

"It's crazy how we came to be, but I want you to know that I love you and appreciate you more than I can say."

"Where'd that come from, Snow?"

"From my heart," I replied honestly.

He smiled at me with all the love he'd given me from the beginning of our relationship. I stood up with my sandwich in hand and walked around my desk to where he sat. He opened his arms and I got comfortable in his lap, before putting my sandwich up to his lips.

"Oh, you sharing?"

"Just take a bite, fool, before I change my mind," I said, forcing him to open his mouth.

He bit it while laughing, and then I did the same. I finished eating while he held me, and we talked about rebuilding our future once this last threat was eliminated. We both still had big dreams, but once Phillisa had gone off of our radar, it had been hard to think about those dreams without looking over both shoulders. Her death would free us in more ways than one. The sounding of an alarm going off interrupted our moment of solace and made me hop up out of his lap.

"What the hell is *that*?" Fatz asked, looking around frantically.

"The alarm that's triggered by someone being within a mile of here," I said, going to my laptop and pulling up all the camera angles I had.

It only took me a few seconds to spot all the cop cars headed towards us.

"Cops are here," I said, pulling the phone towards me and dialing my lawyer's number.

She answered immediately and didn't give me time to talk before she started spitting instructions. I listened intently, and then hung up.

"We gotta go," I said, hitting the intercom buttons and relaying the message for Ace and Junior to come to my office immediately.

"Why are they here, bae?"

"Because my blood was found at the scene, and Phillisa made a statement. Kelsey is working overtime to get me out in front of this, so she suggested I make myself *unavailable* for the moment," I replied, going to the newly installed gun safe.

I pulled out several handguns and grabbed a bag to put them in. I kept the modified AR-27 with the hundred and twenty-round drum out on the desk.

"She said make yourself unavailable, *not* get a breaking news highlight for the ten o'clock news," Fatz said.

"What's going on, Mom?" Junior asked, rushing into the room, with Ace right behind.

I manually shut down the alarm s I could be heard without having to scream.

"The cops will be here in less than sixty seconds, and they'll explain why, which means I don't have to. Fatz and I are going underground to the caves while they do whatever they're gonna do. You already know what to say when they ask for my whereabouts," I said.

"Yeah, just give them Kelsey's number, and let your lawyer handle it from there," Junior replied.

"Exactly. Junior, your retina will get you into anywhere or anything you need in this house or on the property. I'm telling you this, because if we decide to leave the property, you'll be able to defend yourself and Ace. I'll send you a text, but *don't* text me first. I don't know if they're trying to monitor the cell towers in the area right now. I love you," I said, pulling him into my arms for a quick hug.

"I love you too, Mom, and I got everything under control." I passed him off to Fatz, and I turned my attention on Ace.

"Trial by fire, slim, but you're built for this, right?"

"I'm battle tested Snow, so don't worry about me."

I nodded my head before turning and picking up my bag and gun and heading for the bookcase that contained the elevator. By the time I scanned my retina to open the elevator Fatz was back by my side, and we boarded together.

"Be safe, Mom."

"Always, son. I'll see you in a minute," I said, winking at him.

The doors shut on his smile, and we made the descent into the darkness.

"So, are they coming with an actual warrant, or is this the question-and-answer portion?" he asked.

"As deep as they were, I doubt they just wanted to chit chat. My blood being on that asphalt proves that I was there, but it doesn't prove *why* I was there. I don't know what Phillisa said to them, but I'm hoping it's something to incriminate me."

"Wait, what? You're *hoping* it's something to incriminate you? Why?" he asked, perplexed.

"Because it only makes her look worse when the DNA comes out."

He nodded in understanding, as the door opened on the ground floor. I hadn't done a lot of remodeling down here, mainly because once you reached this level, it was all about getting to the boats. I'd made the lighting better and made sure the ground was leveled in a way that prevented spraining an ankle if you had to run.

"Let's go to the boat, and we can monitor the house cameras from there," I said.

He took the gun from my hand and used the strap to sling it over his shoulder so he could hold my hand as we walked. We walked down the middle tunnel and came to the dock where the speed boat was waiting. The sleek, all-black, twenty-two hundred horsepower bullet of a speed boat had cost three million dollars, but it was worth every cent. It was luxurious, and faster than anything on the open market to date, with its fiberglass and aluminum alloy build. I'd named it Ghost when I'd bought it a few years back, and despite the lack of seat time to test drive it, I was still counting on it to perform beautifully.

"After you, my lady," Fatz said, bowing in exaggeration and mockery of an English gentleman.

My laughter led the way as we climbed on board and went below to the single master cabin. I quickly pulled out my phone and brought the security system online. The cops were still at the front gate, and from the looks of it, they were pissed because Junior was talking to them through the intercom. I couldn't help smiling with pride because my son was a *whole* asshole, just like his parents.

"What's going on?"

"They're still trying to get through the gate," I said, turning my phone so he could see the action.

He laughed along with me. When I turned the phone back around towards me, I saw Junior and Ace walking down to the front gate, with one of the security guards trailing them with a dog. I put the phone down so I could power up the boat and allow the Wi-Fi to connect both mine and Fatz's phones. The sudden sound of a gunshot froze me for a second, and I turned to look at Fatz. It took a few more seconds for me to realize the shot I'd heard hadn't come from nearby, but from my phone. I grabbed it and looked, and what I saw made me drop it right back on the bed.

"What is it, baby?" Fatz asked.

I opened my mouth to speak, but all that came out was air. I couldn't speak, nor could I warn him of what was about to happen. All I could do was collapse.

Aryanna

CHAPTER 15

"Come on, Snow, wake up. Wake up, baby." I could hear Fatz's voice, but it seemed far off for some reason.

I couldn't see him, but I knew to keep moving towards the sound of his voice because that signaled safety.

"That's it, baby, wake up," Fatz said.

I could feel his hands stroking my face lovingly, and this is what made me open my eyes. For a few seconds, I didn't know where I was, but then the decor of the boat registered to my brain.

"Wh-what happened?"

"You passed out," he replied.

"What? Why?"

He didn't immediately respond, and that had me trying to sit up faster than I should've. My vision swam and my stomach lurched, but I didn't throw up. When my vision finally cleared my eyes went straight to my phone on the floor, and my memory flooded back to me.

"Did-did they shoot him?" I asked softly.

"No, but they detained him and took him away. I don't know where yet, but they're up there searching the house right now."

"What the fuck was he *thinking*? Why would he pull a gun and fire a shot? Did he hit anyone?" I asked.

"No, from the looks of things he must've shot in the air, but I don't know why. I waited to reach out to Ace, plus I was worried about you." I smiled sheepishly, while slowly pushing up off of his lap and getting shakily to my feet.

I took a few deep breaths, and once I realized I wasn't gonna vomit, I bent and picked up my phone. I immediately went back to the security footage and watched it all unfold from the beginning. Sure enough I saw Junior standing behind the security guard, arguing, and then he pulled his gun out. His stupid ass was lucky he kept it pointed at the sky when he let a shot off.

I took careful notice of the security guard standing in front of him too, because he deserved one hell of a bonus for standing between my son and certain death.

"I think we should get out of here and go make sure Junior is ok, bae."

"We can't just walk into the station right now, Fatz, but I can put Kelsey on it," I said, already dialing her number.

Her secretary put me straight through, and a few seconds later, I was running down what had transpired. I didn't even finish the story before she agreed to go get him out, and just bill it as part of my case. This was why I paid that premium price for the best legal team money could buy.

"Alright, she's gonna take care of the situation with Junior, so all we have to do is sit and wait," I said, reclaiming my spot in his lap. "What are you doing?"

"I'm not doing anything, bae," I replied, innocently, while snuggling up to him.

The fact that my ass was in his lap didn't escape either of us, just like his growing excitement didn't escape me.

"Snow," he said, making his warning clear by squeezing me around the waist.

"Yes, Andrew?"

I smiled up at him, knowing I was playing with the best kind of fire. The smoldering look in his eyes always did something to me, and made my pussy ache with desire. I didn't wait for him to give in to me though, I wrapped my hand around the back of his neck and pulled his mouth down to mine. Our kiss was equal parts hunger and within seconds, we were pulling at each other's clothing. We ended up naked with me on my back on the bed, and my legs trapping his face in between my thighs. He licked my pussy with so much patience, my legs were trembling by the time his tongue made it to my clit. I felt his teeth graze my pussy lips, and that sent a vibration through my body from head to toe. My hands were tangled in his dreads, but I didn't pull him away from his feast until I could feel my toes start to curl.

"Put that dick in me," I demanded huskily.

He complied immediately, wasting no time climbing on top of me and opening my treasure chest. His first stroke was one of love, so it was tender while still packing a punch. By the third stroke, I was convinced that we were having make-up sex, because his dick was knocking at my stomach lining, trying to make itself at home.

I tried locking my legs around him and pulling him deeper inside me to where I could control him, but he wasn't having that. His short rabbit strokes felt like stiff jabs to my G-spot and that made me cum viciously. When I bit his shoulder, he shook me off, and fucked me harder.

"F-FATZ!" I screamed loudly, clutching onto him as tightly as I could.

He quickly flipped me over onto my stomach, wrapped his hand around my throat, and dove back inside me like an Olympic swimmer. The sound of him growling in my ear made my pussy sing with pleasure, as he built the beat for round two.

"T-take it all daddy," I begged.

I was unable to move or fuck him back, so all I could do was squeeze my pussy muscles like vise grips every time he hit the bottom of my ocean. Wave after wave, the storm inside me got bigger until both of us became the eye of the storm. When his grip tightened on my throat, I came until I was breathless, and he came right behind me. When his cum finally stopped pumping inside me he collapsed on my back. I absorbed his weight willingly, and with a smile of satisfaction on my face.

"I need sleep," I said, yawning sleepily.

He responded by rolling off of me and pulling me onto his chest where I laid my head. I closed my eyes and it seemed like a few seconds before I was drifting off into the land of dreams. In my dreams, I was with Fatz on a beach and we were strolling along hand in hand, without a care in the world. I could feel myself smiling even in my sleep, but I suddenly felt a shadow looking over me. Before I knew it, I was snatched from my sleep, and Fatz was holding me steady.

"It's ok, baby, I'm right here," he whispered, tightening his grip on me.

I looked up into his dark eyes and when I sensed no worries or fear, I laid my head back on his chest. The rhythm of his heartbeat lulled me back into my slumber, but this time there were no dreams waiting for me. When I awoke again, I was still secured in the same position, and Fatz was still asleep. I laid there for a moment, because I had the feeling that something had woke me up. I was just about to dismiss the notion that something was off when I heard noise outside the boat. I tapped Fatz and put my hand over his mouth before he could speak.

"Someone is in the tunnel," I whispered.

He gave a quick nod, and we moved like synchronized dancers in the way we got up to grab our weapons. I pulled my Colt Anaconda .45 revolver out of my bag and moved on Fatz's left side while straining my ears to listen. I thought I might've been tripping, but when I heard movement, I looked at Fatz and I could tell he'd heard it too. He put his finger to his lips, while motioning for me to go low and he was going high. I nodded while inching towards the door with my gun leveled out in front of me.

"Snow," Ace called out.

I let out a sigh of relief and lowered my pistol, while pushing Fatz to the side so Ace didn't get a sneak peek at his dick.

"Bitch, you almost got shot," I said, opening the door.

"I'm sorry, but I tried calling first. The cops are done tossing the house, and I need you two back up there."

"We'll be there in a minute," I replied.

She looked me up and down once, while licking her lips, and then she turned away.

"Why you push me out of the way?"

"Stop playing with me," I replied, turning and pushing him towards the bed.

He laughed and pulled me with him, and before I knew it, I was somehow on my back again with his weight holding me to the mattress.

"Baby, you know she wouldn't have come down here if it wasn't important," I said.

"This is important."

I giggled as he kissed me right below my left tittie and let his tongue trace the wet outline that his lips left. I was tempted to give into his desire, but I knew there was work to do.

"Come on, bae, we gotta go get Junior," I said.

I could feel the reluctance in the way his lips kept up their onslaught, but he eventually pulled back and climbed off me. When he held out his hand I grabbed it, and he pulled me to my feet. We quickly got dressed and made our way back upstairs to my office, where I found Ace waiting.

"What's the deal?" I asked, sitting down behind my desk and looking around at the chaos the cops had left.

"Did you see what happened with Junior and the cops?" she asked.

"Yeah, and why the fuck would he do something so stupid?" Fatz asked.

"To put the focus on him and get their attention off of Snow."

Ace's statement immediately changed my feelings of wanting to kick my son's ass, and when I looked at Fatz, I could see that he'd softened too.

"Ok, well I already put my lawyer on top of it," I said.

"Yeah, well that ain't our only problem. One of the cops who helped flip the house was gay… and cute, and I was kickin it with her while she was supposed to be doing her thang. I pumped her for info of course, and what she said is the cops like you for some unsolved cold cases. Them searching here and trying to detain you was bigger than what happened with your son and—"

"*Don't* call him that," I growled, angrily.

"Sorry. The cops being here was bigger than what we thought," Ace concluded.

"Well, I guess we know what kind of statement Phillisa made," Fatz said.

"Maybe, but did the cops *really* expect to find shit here…or were they planning to *plant* something?" I asked, looking around to see if I noticed anything out of the ordinary.

Both Fatz and Ace immediately picked up on the fact that we now had to proceed like this was an unsecured environment to talk. I put my finger up to prevent either of them from any further talking as I turned to my laptop on my desk. I quickly logged into the security system and ran a complete diagnostic on the entire property to see if any new surveillance equipment had been installed. While we waited on that, I sent a message to Kelsey, inquiring about how soon we could get Junior out.

When my computer started beeping, I focused my undivided attention on the screen, reading and then rereading what was there. When I was satisfied, I proceeded with the conversation.

"There's no new listening devices in the house, so we're good," I said.

"So, what's our next move?" Ace asked.

"How friendly did you get with the cop that told you this shit?" I countered.

"I mean, I got the number, and I can pull up whenever."

"Good, because I want you to pull up on her tonight and put it down, so that she falls in love with your ass. You know what to do after that," I said.

"Is there anything you're looking for in particular when it comes to information?" she asked.

"Nah, just keep your ears open. The clearer the vision of God that you bring her through climax, the more freely she'll confess," I said.

"Church," Fatz chimed in.

Ace chuckled as she pulled her phone out and started texting.

"I'm gonna go through the house and check out the damage. You wanna join me?" Fatz asked.

"Sure," I replied.

I shut down my laptop and followed him out of the office. We went room to room, making a mental checklist of things that were broken or damaged. By the time we made it back to my office, I was ready to find out who led the way when it came to this search, so I could put a price on his or her head.

"We could leave, but it doesn't really make sense to, because we can always hide if or when the cops come back," Fatz said.

"Yeah, but how long do you think it'll be before Phillisa remembers the tunnels and tips the police to that?"

He nodded in agreement and understanding, which meant that we now had to way the pros and cons of staying versus running. Even if the cops knew about the tunnels, they still didn't know how to get into them through the house, and the water was protected by boobytraps. At the same time, I didn't wanna have to live in a place where I was just waiting for the door to be kicked in.

"Do you remember those properties I had Mo buy before... before shit went sideways?" I asked, looking at Fatz closely.

"Yeah."

"Well, they were in her name, and I know she didn't have any family she was close enough with to leave shit to. So, what do you think happened to everything?" I asked.

"More than likely, it reverted back to the bank, but even if it didn't, we're *not* going anywhere near them."

The determination was clear to see in his eyes and I knew better than to press the issue, so I left it alone.

"Alright, I've got a date with Officer Angela Wilson," Ace said, coming back into the office.

"I'll run her name by my people and find out what makes her tick," I said, seizing the opportunity to move away from the conversation Fatz and I had been having.

I went back behind my desk and hopped back on my laptop.

"I'm gonna find somewhere for us to relocate too," Fatz said, leaving the room.

My instinct was to go to him and smooth the feathers I'd obviously ruffled, but I chose to leave it alone for now. Ace took a seat across from me and waited patiently while I reached out to various people.

I was still working on my computer and my phone an hour later, when the buzzer for the front gate sounded off. When I checked the cameras I was surprised to see my lawyer's face staring back at me. I wasted no time buzzing her through, and then I sent Ace to escort her in. When Kelsey walked into my office, I sized her up from head to toe, trying to read her body language. She was all polish in her navy-blue skirt suit with matching six-inch stilettos.

Her beauty was undeniable, because it was natural in the way that little makeup is required to enhance it. Her skin was a sun-kissed bronze, her hair was dark brown with blonde highlights, and her shape was sexy curvy. Normally, the first thing I'd see is that infectious smile of hers, but she was all business right now and that worried me slightly.

"I wasn't expecting you, Kelsey," I said.

"And I wasn't anticipating having to bring you bad news face-to-face, but..."

"Whatever it is just spit it out, because taking your time won't make it better," I said, bracing for impact.

"Junior is in the hospital. He was stabbed not long after getting to the county jail."

Aryanna

CHAPTER 16

"What did you say?" I asked softly.

"Claudette, I'm so sorry. I tried to get him out as fast as I could, but I found this out while I was trying to get his bond figured out," Kelsey said.

For a second my mind went blank, as I imagined my son once again laid up in somebody's hospital, fighting for his life.

"How the fuck did Phillisa get to him so fast?" I growled through clenched teeth.

"What's going on?" Fatz asked, walking into the office.

Our eyes locked and I don't know what he saw in mine, but within an instant he was by my side, with my hand clasped in between both of his.

"Baby, what is it?"

"Jun-Junior got stabbed, and he's in the hospital," I mumbled, while fighting the emotional avalanche that was trying to swallow me.

"*What! How?*" Fatz asked, turning his attention on Kelsey.

"It wasn't my fault, I did everything I could to get him out, but this situation had to have literally been going on simultaneously," she replied defensively.

"No one is blaming you, Kelsey, we're just trying to understand the timeline," I stated.

"I figured that and that's why I asked all the questions I could before I got here. All I was able to find out is that he was in the holding tank, and one of the cops called his name to tell him I'd be down soon to see him. One of the guys in the tank with him said two black guys asked him his name after that, and when he repeated it, they immediately jumped on him," Kelsey said.

I processed this information quietly, while considering all the meanings behind it. My son hadn't been out here since he was a kid, and he *definitely* hadn't done shit to make a name for himself back then. I, on the other hand, had absolutely made a name for myself, and it rang enough bells to get my whole family line annihilated.

Even knowing that though, I still didn't think that's what caused Junior to get stabbed. My gut said it was the name he shared with his dad that had caused this traumatic situation.

"What hospital is he in?" I asked.

"Dade County General, but Snow, you *cannot* show your face right now. I've done the best smear campaign I can with the information you provided, so now we have to wait and let it play out," Kelsey replied.

"I'll go," Ace volunteered.

When I looked up at Fatz, I could see the longing in him to be by my son's side, but I also saw the intelligence and I knew based on that, we both had to sit this one out.

"Go ahead, Ace, but I'm sending some people with you to guard the hospital," I said.

"Understood," she replied.

"Is Junior free on bond, despite being in the hospital?" Fatz asked.

"He is and I suggest you move him as soon as the doctor gives the ok," Kelsey replied.

I immediately got on my phone and got my people ready to meet Ace at the hospital. My next move was to make travel plans to send Junior back to Colorado with Alexia and Asad, because I couldn't have him out here on the front line with me. The thought of him dying was too distracting for me, and therefore he was a liability.

"You know he's not gonna go quietly, right?" Fatz asked.

"He doesn't got a fucking choice! I'm not about to lose my son."

I knew how heartless this sounded, considering the fact that I'd just put a bullet in the head of a child I'd given birth to. I didn't care though. All I cared about was everyone I loved making it out of this situation alive.

"Ace, you can go to the hospital, and I want you to escort Junior to the airport. Once you all are on the plane, I want you to call me," I said.

"Wait, you want me to leave with him?"

"You can come back once he's settled, but nine times out of ten, there won't be a reason for you to come back. Fatz and I will be good," I replied, looking pointedly at him.

He gave me a nod of understanding, and that was all I needed. I could tell Ace wanted to argue, but she simply nodded as she stood up and left the room.

"Kelsey, I want you to do me a favor. I want you to call a press conference and expose the fact of who that child was to me. Offer up five million for the conviction of his killer, and post Phillisa's picture with it. This should speed up the smear campaign," I said.

"You're the boss, Snow," she said, getting up and leaving.

With just me and Fatz in the room, we communicated silently for a moment. I knew the fears he felt without him saying anything and they were something we shared. I knew he had my back like I had his, and that was all that mattered at the end of the day.

"Do you got a plan?" he asked.

"As soon as I get her location, I will. But in the meantime, we apply pressure to force her out of her hiding spot."

"What about the situation with Gunz? I know he's gone, but do you think we need to scorch the earth to make sure none of his minions follow?" he asked.

I thought about this for a moment, and I knew what I'd normally do.

"We can't spare the manpower, nor can we give it our full attention, so we leave it unless it becomes an issue."

"I got you. What's our next move?" he asked.

I thought about it from a logical standpoint and not an emotional one. I knew I'd have to go to the cops sooner or later and answer their questions, but the plan was for them to view me as a victim and not a suspect. Until I was sure I was being viewed in that light, I had every intention of staying out of sight.

"We need to find a safe place to lay low until the tide turns," I said.

"We could always take that trip to Colorado with Junior and Ace."

His suggestion made me look at him closely for an ulterior motive, but I didn't detect anything disingenuous. That made me consider it seriously for a second.

"We don't know that Phillisa doesn't have people watching us, and for that reason, I don't wanna run the risk of leading her back to the kids," I replied.

He nodded without any argument, but that put us right back in the same position. Despite how I'd had to live my life in the last decade, I still wasn't used to running from anyone. Maybe the best solution was to run and take Phillisa with us.

"I've got a crazy idea, bae."

"What?" he asked, cautiously.

"Let's go to Columbia."

The look on his face told me *exactly* what he thought of that idea, but I still waited on him to speak.

"You're *not* serious, Claudette. Why the hell would we commit suicide by going to the *one place* this bitch is bulletproof?"

"Because there's no way she has been forgiven for turning Campa over to me, which means her support is probably not what you think it is. We might be able to set a trap for her to fall into," I said.

"I'm listening, so break it down for me how you think this is gonna work."

"Well, if we lure her over there, with the intention of handing her to the Columbians to kill her, I think that might satisfy them. What do you think?" I asked.

He considered the question silently, and I let him take as long as he needed.

"I think you *might* have a point, but it's still a gamble bae. If it goes wrong, it's gonna go *real wrong*, plus there's no guarantee you can get the Columbians to listen. So, I just need you to know and recognize that."

"Understood. I'll make the arrangements," I replied, immediately going to my phone's contacts.

He nodded and took the seat across from me, while pulling out his own phone. Securing the travel arrangements was easy, but when it came to how to get into the country to have a sit-down *without* getting shot, that was more difficult.

I'd made a few contacts in Columbia, outside of the sit-down I'd had with Phillisa and her people, but it seemed like nobody could get close enough to request the sit-down with the cartel. I greased as many palms as I could though, and I accepted I had to leave the rest up to luck and fate.

"The plane is ready," he said, looking across the desk at me.

"Have Ace and Junior left yet?"

His fingers went to work rapidly on his phone, and a few moments later he gave me a thumbs up.

"Alright then, let's get this show on the road," I said, standing up.

I sent a quick text to my driver, letting him know he was free for the next seven days. With that done, I led the way back to the entrance that led to the elevator. This time when we got to the caves, we didn't stop to make memories having sex, we went straight to the boat and pushed out into open waters. A half an hour later we docked, and four of my men met us. We piled into the waiting SUVs and sped away into the night.

"When we get on the plane, we'll FaceTime with the kids," I said.

"Are we telling them where we're going?"

"No...we're saying goodbye without them knowing it," I replied honestly.

I expected him to say something, but instead he reached out into the darkness, took my hand, and pulled me towards him. My mind had been focusing on the kiss I knew was coming, but the feeling of a bullet breathing its fire inches from my ear changed that. The sound came milliseconds later, but Fatz was already folding his body over mine. Even with the sounds being muffled, I still knew what automatic gunfire was and the way our truck was rocking only confirmed my assessment.

"Go around them or through them!" Fatz hollered.

The SUV swerved wildly and then picked up speed rapidly. I tried pushing Fatz off of me, but he had me pinned between the seat and the floorboard of the truck.

"Fatz, let me up to shoot," I demanded.

He didn't respond, but he didn't move, so I was forced to stay put.

I could still hear gunfire being exchanged, but it was becoming more distant with each second. It seemed like an eternity before the truck finally came to a stop, and the doors were flung open.

"Fatz," I said, pushing against him when he hesitated to get off of me.

One minute I was smothered and the next thing I knew Fatz wasn't on me, and I could move. I hopped up and quickly exited the truck while pulling my gun out. I was surprised to find myself standing in the parking lot of the Dade County hospital. When I looked back to see which one of my men was hurt, I dropped my gun.

"Fatz," I mumbled weakly.

Before I could take a step towards his prone figure on the ground, there were hospital workers surrounding him and lifting him up onto a stretcher.

"F-Fatz," I said, choking on the sob bubbling up in my throat.

His silence hurt my soul, but even more frightening than that was the crimson stain spreading across his back. The nurses didn't bother strapping him to the stretcher, they simply took off at a full sprint towards the hospital.

"Ms. Snow, we need to get you somewhere safe."

I turned to find two of my men standing in front of me and one of them was holding my gun out to me.

"I can't leave him," I replied hollowly.

"With all due respect, Ms. Snow, the police have probably already been called, and we still don't know where or who the enemy is that attacked us."

I took my gun from his outstretched hand, put it to his head and pulled the trigger.

"I'm not leaving him," I said, looking squarely into the eyes of the man standing to my left.

"I'll get more men here and we'll lock down the hospital Ms. Snow," he replied readily.

I nodded my head and tucked my gun into my waistline while stepping over the dead body in front of me. I walked into the hospital in a daze, feeling colder inside than I'd ever felt in my life. Seeing Fatz on that ground had shifted something in my soul, and it was a feeling unlike anything I'd yet experienced.

"Which room did they take that man in, the one on the stretcher with the gunshot wound?" I asked the nurse sitting behind the desk at the nurse's station.

"He went straight into surgery, so you'll have to wait down here for him."

"Where is the surgery room? He's my husband and he needs to know I'm here," I said.

"I'm sorry ma'am, but you really cannot go into the operating room. If you would just have a seat over there and—"

Her words suddenly got stuck in her throat when the cold steel of my revolver touched her forehead.

"Last time I'm asking," I said softly.

"D-down the hall," she replied shakily.

I heard the gasps from people around me, but I didn't give a fuck about who saw me put a gun to someone's head. I concealed my pistol under my shirt, before heading in the direction the kind nurse had given me.

I had to check three different rooms before I came upon the one Fatz was in. I tried to walk in the room but seeing him laid out on the operating table sent my mind in a tailspin to the time Asad had gotten shot. That night had been an emotional rollercoaster, but it was *nothing* compared to what I was feeling right now.

My heart felt like it would seize up from fear alone at any moment. I watched through the small window in the door, helpless and as frightened as I'd ever been to lose someone in my life. Not even Zion's death had gripped me with otherworldly panic the way this experience was. I worked to take deep breaths and tried to quiet the screaming in my mind.

I'd almost found the resting place between calm and numb when the unthinkable happened. I pushed open the doors to the surgery room and stepped into my worst nightmare.

"We're losing him! Begin chest compressions!" the doctor ordered.

Everyone was moving so fast and paying so much attention to Fatz, no one even knew I was in the room. I stopped a few feet away from him because I couldn't take my eyes off of his face. He was still and peaceful enough to have been sleeping, until his whole body convulsed under the electric shock they hit him with to restart his heart. The loud ringing of him flat lining echoed off every wall in the room and it seemed to make my own heart refuse to beat.

"Clear," the doctor ordered before hitting Fatz with the electric paddles again.

I prayed for the ringing to stop, and then I realized it wouldn't until his heart started. I wanted to scream at them to help him, but I knew that would only serve to distract them at a crucial moment. So, I kept my mouth shut. I had no idea how long they kept working because at some point, I stopped seeing what was in front of me.

My mind rewound time to Dubai and I was remembering all the moments Fatz and I had created together. I could see every smile he put on my face and every moment he made my heart flutter like a schoolgirl's. The good times we had far outweighed the bad ones, and my mind was grasping at those now, like a person in the desert dying of thirst.

Just as quickly as I'd slipped into this state of being, I was forced out of it by a sudden silence. The ringing had stopped in my ears, but it wasn't until I saw no one moving that I understood why that was.

Aryanna

CHAPTER 17

"Ma'am, you can't be in here," the nurse said, approaching me.

"My husband," I mumbled.

"I understand...and I'm so sorry for your loss, but you can't be in here right now," she insisted.

I looked at her standing in front of me, but I wasn't really seeing her. In this moment, she was just someone who had taken something from me, like so many others had. It wasn't a conscious thought for me to shoot her, but when I saw her eyes bulge from the barrel being pressed into the flesh of her forehead, I knew what had to happen. I pulled the trigger and before her body dropped, I had the gun swinging in the direction of the doctor.

"Pl-please don't hurt us. It won't bring your husband back and—"

He never got to finish his plea before my gun barked and sprayed his brain matter all over the nurse behind him. The three remaining nurses huddled together, which made targeting them easier. I shot each one of them in the head before the begging could start and then went to Fatz's side.

I'd seen death on many faces before, but he somehow didn't look dead. He didn't look asleep like I'd thought earlier when they'd been trying to save his life. All I could think was that he looked beautiful, and he looked like he missed me. I climbed up on the operating table with him and despite the blood, I still laid my head on his chest. I could feel the tears leaking from my eyes, but no sound came from my mouth. For once in my life, I was speechless, and it was the immense pain that made me this way.

"I-l love you so much, baby. I don't know how to do this without you, but I promise to try."

The sound of the door opening made me sit up with my gun outstretched and aiming.

"We gotta go, Ms. Snow, the police are here and they're trying to surround the hospital."

I started to pull the trigger and eject the thought he just had through the hole in his ear, but I controlled my rage. I didn't wanna leave Fatz now, any more than I had Tony when Campa had murdered him, but I knew there was no way to quickly exit with his body.

"I'll come back for you, my love. I promise," I whispered, kissing Fatz's lips gently.

The heat still harnessed within him gave me the strength I needed to get down off the table and walk away. I could feel the pull of his heart calling to me, even though it had ceased to beat in tune with my own. Fatz was inside me and I knew that, just as surely as I knew he'd been the one God had made for me.

"Lead the way," I said.

As soon as we came out of the operating room, I could hear the sound of walkie talkies echoing throughout the corridor. I tucked my gun and walked with purpose, while trying not to bring attention to myself. We went out a side door, and there was a black SUV waiting for us. I quickly hopped into the back, and we sped out of the hospital's back entrance. I could see the front of the hospital was awash with flashing red and blue lights, even from my position, which signaled the amount of cops on the scene.

I had every intention of honoring the promise I'd just made Fatz, but in my heart I knew if I got into a shootout with the cops, I wouldn't mind reuniting with him in the afterlife. I kept my eyes trained out the side window, not really seeing anything, while trying to figure out my next move. I'd been the one to suggest Columbia to Fatz, but going without him didn't seem like the right thing to do. All I knew for sure was that Phillisa had to die, and she had to die *gruesomely*.

First, I needed to figure out how she was able to ambush us. Logical deduction told me the reason I'd gotten by the cops searching my house without them searching the tunnels, was because Phillisa had kept that little secret. She must've had her men laying on me, figuring I'd come out that way. My predictably had more than likely gotten Fatz killed, and that was something I had to live with. The question was how would I ever be able to explain this to my kids?

Fatz was as much a part of their lives as he was mine. Hell, he'd been more of a dad to Junior than Zion had been given a chance to be. I didn't yet know how I was gonna explain this loss to them, but I knew it had to be done in person.

"Take me to the airport," I demanded.

"Right away, Ms. Snow."

I pulled my phone out and sent Ace a message to let her know I was flying out right behind her, and to tell the kids I'd be there as soon as I could. It took thirty minutes to get to the airport, but once I was secured on the plane, time stopped existing for me. I knew sleep was an impossibility, so I didn't even try chasing that demon. I simply laid my head back and closed my eyes.

Fatz was there when I did. I could see his smile and feel the warmth it brought me in my heart. It amazed me that I'd known love with Zion, but what Fatz had given me was so much more. Its purity defined how rare it was, and that's what made me cherish it for every moment I'd had it. He and I didn't waste a minute when it came to loving each other, because we both understood how fleeting and precious life was. I'd never be able to thank him enough for living life like that with me, but I was more than eternally grateful.

In this moment, my sanity was rooted in the memories my mind was producing. Before I knew it, I could feel the plane descending through the clouds, signaling our arrival to Colorado. I knew I was gonna have to relocate everyone because it wasn't safe to be here anymore, and I wouldn't risk my kid's lives on the *maybe* that Phillisa had forgot this spot. My kids were all I had left in this world, and I would hold onto them as tight as I could.

When the plane touched down and taxied into the private hanger, we were met by two SUVs. I got off the plane and hopped in without a second thought, and I immediately found myself looking down a gun barrel.

"Don't think about reaching for your weapon, Ms. Snow, because I've been given permission to kill you if I have to," the young Colombian said, turning in the passenger seat to face me.

I heard two gunshots and then the back door across from me opened. Another young Colombian slid onto the seat beside me and quickly frisked me until he found my gun. I felt naked as soon as he took it from me, but I showed no signs of panic.

"Where is she?" I asked.

"You'll see soon enough... if you cooperate," the man in the front seat replied.

I sat back and looked bored while staring out the window. Internally, my mind was racing as I tried to figure a way out of this shit, because I *refused* to accept that I was gonna let my kids lose their whole family in one day. The drive up into the mountains was different than ever before for a lot of reasons, but the fact that Fatz wasn't sitting next to me was the main thing on my mind. I closed my eyes and prayed silently, not to God, but to Fatz.

I prayed that the force of nature he was, would somehow guide me in what was coming closer, with every passing mile. I didn't get some sudden epiphany, but I did get a feeling of calm that flowed over and through me. I focused on that for the entire hour and a half ride, and by the time we came to a stop, I had something like an idea rolling around my brain.

"Let's go," my escort said, opening my door, and stepping back so I couldn't lunge for his gun.

I hopped out and followed his lead into my house. When we came through the front door, I knew instantly that Phillisa was here. It was like I could *feel* that bitch, and all I wanted was to sever her head so I could put it on my coffee table! I knew to bide my time though and have faith in my man.

"Is that you, Snow? We're in the kitchen having banana splits," Phillisa called out.

I followed the sound of her voice around a corner and came face-to-face with my greatest enemy. She was sitting at the table calmly with a pistol beside her bowl of ice cream. I took a quick survey of the room, counting four more Columbian hittas. Ace was laying on the floor, unconscious or possibly dead, if the blood leaking from her head was any indication.

I didn't see Alexia at first, and that put my heart in my stomach, but then I realized she was standing in the corner behind Asad. When my eyes met Asad's, there was so much pain and confusion, I felt physically ill about the truth coming out like this. There was no turning back the hands of time though, which meant I had to push through this in order to push past his pain.

"What's wrong, Snow? You don't look too happy to see me," Phillisa said.

"On the contrary, I'm so glad to see you because now I don't have to go far to kill your bitch ass," I replied, smiling.

"Kill me? Would you really murder me in front of my son, Snow? Wait, what am I talking about, you murdered your *own son*, so I know your moral compass is fucked up."

"He wasn't my son bitch, he was a product of your father's raping me. You knew that and you *still* raised him as your son. So, I didn't kill *my* son, I killed yours," I replied.

"Well, it's a good thing for you that I'm a better woman than you are, and I try not to kill kids. Did you notice I said *try*...which brings about the question of Junior. Don't you wanna know where Junior is?"

Her taunting only increased my hate for her, but I maintained my cool.

"I know Junior ain't dead, you silly bitch," I said, smiling.

"Oh yeah? I think you're bluffing and *praying* I didn't hurt your baby boy."

"He's not my baby boy," I said, still smiling while looking over at Asad.

My statement made her pick her pistol up and aim it at me.

"I'm Claudette Snow, bitch. I don't flinch and you know that."

"You may be Claudette Snow, but bitch, that don't make you bulletproof," Phillisa said.

"You're right, I ain't bulletproof, but that don't mean I ain't protected. I move with the angels, and I've got plenty of them watching over me."

"Like who? Zion?" she asked, laughing.

"Sure, he's one of them. I know you think he loved you and maybe he did, Phillisa, but he was *in love* with me. I used to hate you, because I blamed you for breaking up my family, and for getting Zion killed by your father. I don't hate you for that anymore though...and I haven't, ever since I got to know Asad. He's the blessing that came with all the chaos and carnage," I said, smiling at him.

I felt the pain in my leg before the sound of the gunshot reached my ears. Luckily for me, I fell backwards into the wall, which kept me from attacking the kitchen floor. It hurt like shit to get shot, but I refused to cry out for her. I'd bite my tongue off first.

"Your aim sucks, bitch," I growled through clenched teeth.

The barrel of her gun rose higher until we were winking at each other.

"Stop," Asad said, taking a step towards Phillisa.

"Stay out of this, Asad, this is grown folk's business," Phillisa said, looking down the barrel at me.

"I said stop."

This time when Asad gave that instruction, he followed it up by pulling a gun out and putting it to his mom's head. Phillisa's men responded immediately by pulling out their own guns.

"Have you lost your goddamn mind, boy? Get that gun off me!" she raged.

"Put yours down first, and don't think about shooting my mom again."

"Asad, *I'm your mom*! She fucking kidnapped you from me and told you I was dead! *I'm your mom!*"

"You're right, you're my biological mother, but Snow has raised me for the last ten years. She's taken care of me when I was sick, and whooped my ass when I needed it, so she's my mother in every sense of the word. Now, *take your gun off of her*," he demanded, with a cold fury in his voice.

"You turned my son against me, bitch, but you can't have him. He's *my son*," she said, still aiming her gun at my face.

"I'm sorry I was a better mom than you, and Fatz was a better dad. Why don't you look Asad in the face and tell him you took his father from him *again*," I said.

As badly as I hated to hurt my son, I knew exactly what the truth would do to him. I'd decided on the ride up here that the truth was the weapon I had, because if Fatz and I had done nothing else, we'd shown our kids the importance of love and loyalty.

"F-Fatz is dead?" Asad asked softly, looking at me.

I'd been suppressing my feelings of loss, but the devastation on my son's face opened up the floodgates, and the tears came again.

"Yes, sweetheart, he's dead. He died shielding me from the bullets your mother's hittas sent my way."

"Is-is she lying?" Asad asked.

Phillisa didn't answer, she simply stared at me with more hate than could be explained by words.

"Mom," Asad said, looking at me, and letting the tears roll down his cheeks.

"I wish I were lying, baby, but I'm not. I'm so sorry," I said sincerely.

"No-no-no, please God, no," Alexia said, sinking to the floor as she held her stomach.

I wanted to go to her, but the bullet in my leg, and the threat of another one, kept me rooted in my spot.

"He was a casualty of war, Asad, and this is a war I didn't start. Snow started it, but as soon as you get your gun off of me, I'll make her pay for what she's done. We can do it together," Phillisa said.

"How did I start this, Phillisa? I don't recall asking you to get pregnant by my very married husband. If you would've kept your legs closed, then *none* of this would've happened."

"So, what you're saying is that you wish my son had never been born?" Phillisa asked.

"Don't put words in my mouth, bitch."

My speech seemed slurred to my ears, and when I looked down, I saw the blood pumping from my wound. There was little doubt in my mind, I'd pass out sooner than later.

"Where's Junior?" I asked, looking at Asad.

"In the bedroom, handcuffed to the bed. I couldn't stop her," he replied sheepishly, while wiping tears from his eyes.

"Asad, get your gun off of me," Phillisa growled.

"Let me shoot her," Alexia said, stepping forward, and trying to take the gun from Asad.

I could tell they were about to make a huge mistake for all of us.

"You two stop it, and *stay focused*," I insisted.

Of course, they ignored me, which emboldened the man closest to them to make his move. I thought Asad didn't see him coming, but at the last minute he jerked his arm away from Alexia and turned the gun on the advancing man. Two quick taps of the trigger stopped him cold and before Phillisa could try to move, he had the gun pressed to the back of her head again.

"*I got this*, Lexy, just go check on Junior. If any man tries to stop you, I'll push a bullet through the back of her skull," he declared, looking around to make his point felt.

Asad was my baby boy, but right now he was something more than that. He was Zion's son.

Aryanna

CHAPTER 18

"You're not gonna shoot me, Asad. I know you're not gonna shoot me, son, because I gave you life. I carried you inside me for nine months, and protected you every step of the way. I raised you for your first five years of life, Asad, and I would've been here for the last ten years, had I been able to find you. Everything I've done has been for you, son, is because I knew you weren't dead. I knew in my *heart* you weren't dead, and I held onto that hope for the last decade. Please put the gun down, son, and come home with me," Phillisa said, turning around slowly to face Asad.

This movement took the gun from the back of her head to her forehead, and I knew that was her intention, because it made it harder for him to pull the trigger.

"Asad, I'm not saying you have to shoot her, because she *is* the woman who gave birth to you... But she doesn't mean you any good. The reason I took you from her is because I knew it was what your dad would've wanted. I knew Zion better than anyone ever could've, and I knew what was in his heart. He wanted you to grow up happy, healthy, and loved. Not raised by the goons employed by Phillisa. So, you don't have to shoot her, son, you can walk away with me and the rest of your family," I said sincerely.

"They're *not* your family, Asad! I'm your family, and I can't let you go anywhere with a woman who is cold enough to murder her *own son* in cold blood."

I wanted to argue against the bullshit Phillisa was trying to use to fill Asad's head, but I suddenly felt the need to sit down. I could feel my body sliding down the wall, and before I knew it, I was sitting in a pool of my own blood.

"Mom!" Asad said loudly.

I could see the concern in his eyes, but I didn't want him to be distracted right now.

"I'm fine, sweetie, it just hurts to stand up," I said, forcing a smile on my face.

"She's not being truthful, Asad. She's dying, which means you have to choose between keeping that gun on me or getting her some help," Phillisa said.

"Give me your gun," Asad demanded, holding his free hand out towards her.

She hesitated but in the end, she did what he told her to do. He quickly levelled the gun at one of her men, and I could see the determination in his eyes as clearly as I used to see it in Zion.

"Take your belt off, loop it around her thigh, and pull it as tight as you can get it. *Now!*" Asad ordered.

The man came closer to me, moving slow so he wouldn't get shot. He took his belt off and followed the instructions he'd been given.

"Ahhh!" I screamed when he pulled the belt tight.

"Asad, I'll let Snow live if you just come away with me. I know she means a lot to you, so I'll spare her life," Phillisa said.

"Like-like you tried to spare it earlier tonight? Or like you tried to spare it in Dubai when Junior g-got shot? You're lying, Phillisa, and Asad is smarter than to believe your bullshit," I said, wiping away the sweat that was dripping in my eye, and causing it to sting.

"Asad, I give you my word, son. I won't kill her and all you have to do is come home with me where you belong. I just want you back," Phillisa insisted.

I could see the confusion in his eyes now, and I hurt for him. I wouldn't make this harder on him and keep asking him to choose though. At first, I thought I'd had to, but now I saw the pain this moment was causing him, and I didn't want any more of that.

"Asad, I'm sorry for any harm I caused you... but I can't be sorry for wanting to give you the life I knew your father would've wanted. I can't apologize for loving you because you changed my life, and I'm so grateful to call you my son. No matter which one of us gave birth to you, I'll always consider you my son. I love you... and I'll always love you," I said.

He didn't say anything, but the tears in his eyes swiftly built until they spilled over in an endless stream. His pain bled in the rivers that ran from his eyes, and I hurt too because I knew I was failing him by not protecting him. I'd let this bitch hurt him yet again with her selfishness.

"Mom! Mom, are you ok?" Junior asked.

I looked to my left and saw him coming through the doorway, straight to me.

"I'm fine, it's just a flesh wound," I said, smiling up at him.

Junior immediately dropped to his knees and inspected my wound like he'd gone to medical school. I held my breath when he touched me and I somehow managed not to come unglued in the process.

"It's bleeding too much to be a flesh wound, Mom. I think the bullet nicked your artery, which means we need to get you to a hospital," Junior said.

I tried to sit up straight, but the pain was too intense.

"We gotta get you to a doctor," Junior said.

"I need a hospital. I wanna make sure the baby is ok," I replied.

"What baby?" Junior and Asad asked in unison.

"That bitch ain't pregnant, she's lying to save her life and make you feel sorry for her, Asad," Phillisa said aggressively.

"That's not my kind of lie," I replied, smiling.

Asad actually smiled at me and looked down at my stomach. Phillisa said something in rapid Spanish, and her men suddenly went for their guns. I didn't have the chance to warn Asad, but the way he moved let me know that I didn't have to. He raised both guns and put hot holes in both men without hesitation. Phillisa used the distraction to make her move, pushing Asad off balance and springing up out of the chair.

When Asad fell back, Phillisa dove for the gun that had fallen from her dead man's hand, and then she spun in my direction. The hate in her eyes was brighter than a stoplight in the middle of the night and it was blazing at me. I had just enough strength to push Junior out of the way and I stared death in the face like a real gangsta should.

"See you soon, bitch," I said smiling.

She gave no audible response, but she did return my smile, just before flame spit from the barrel and the gun roared emotionally. In moments like this, it wasn't just my life that flashed before my eyes, it was the lives of those I'd touched. I'd meant it when I'd said Asad was my son, because the moment I'd saved his life when he was five years old, I'd taken *responsibility* for his life. It ceased to matter how he'd been conceived, and all that mattered was that he got to live a good life.

Right now, I was more grateful for him than anything in life. The screams that suddenly erupted from Phillisa's mouth were the sweetest sounds I'd heard since Junior was born. I struggled to get to my feet with Junior's help, and by the time I made it, Asad was standing over Phillisa with the barrel of his smoking gun pointed at her.

"Y-you shot me! You shot your own *mother*!" she cried.

"That probably makes us even, if your habit has been to send hittas at Snow," he replied, raising his shirt and showing his mom the scars from his own gunshot wounds.

"You ungrateful puta! *I gave you life!*" Phillisa screamed.

"Thank you," he replied, tapping the trigger twice, and silencing her forever.

Aryanna

CHAPTER 19

Eight Months Later

Brazil

"Mom, he looks just like you," Junior said.

"I think he looks like Fatz, honestly," Asad countered.

"Either way, he's as handsome as his nephew," Alexia chimed in.

"How weird is it gonna be for Zion the third to be older than his own uncle?" Junior asked.

"It's only by a week, so the teasing shouldn't be too bad. Plus, being younger don't mean shit when it comes to handling the important things in life. It was *me* who saved Mom's life that night in Colorado, and all Junior did was carry her to the car," Asad said, laughing.

Everyone except for Junior laughed, but even as he glared at his little brother, there was love and respect in his eyes. All three of my older kids could argue about absolutely everything under the sun, but at the end of the day they were bound by love and loyalty.

"Have you picked a name yet, Mom?" Alexia asked.

I looked down at the sleeping bundle of joy in my arms, and silently took in all of his tiny features one at a time. Fatz had always thought he was an ugly nigga with swag, so it broke my heart that he wasn't standing beside me to witness the beauty we'd created. I knew he could see his son though, and I knew he loved him as much as I did.

"He'll be named after his father, but we'll call him Drew for short," I replied, smiling.

"Drew... yeah, Dad would've liked that," Alexia said.

The emotion in her voice made me look up at her, and the tears in her eyes were clear to see. There wasn't a day that had gone by that we didn't miss Fatz, and it was a pain we all shared. It would never go away...and it probably wouldn't even become the dull ache that was manageable.

We would deal with it together though, and we would let the next generation bring the joy back to our lives. The game never changed, people lived to die. All we could do was live our best lives until our number was called, and make every moment count in between...

The End...

Submission Guideline

Submit the first three chapters of your completed manuscript to ldpsubmissions@gmail.com, subject line: Your book's title. The manuscript must be in a .doc file and sent as an attachment. Document should be in Times New Roman, double spaced and in size 12 font. Also, provide your synopsis and full contact information. If sending multiple submissions, they must each be in a separate email.

Have a story but no way to send it electronically? You can still submit to LDP/Ca$h Presents. Send in the first three chapters, written or typed, of your completed manuscript to:

LDP: Submissions Dept
Po Box 944
Stockbridge, Ga 30281

DO NOT send original manuscript. Must be a duplicate.

Provide your synopsis and a cover letter containing your full contact information.

Thanks for considering LDP and Ca$h Presents.

<u>NEW RELEASES</u>

FRIEND OR FOE 3 by MIMI
A GANGSTA'S KARMA by FLAME
NIGHTMARE ON SILENT AVE by CHRIS GREEN
THE STREETS MADE ME 3 by LARRY D. WRIGHT
MOBBED UP 3 by KING RIO
JACK BOYZ N DA BRONX 3 by ROMELL TUKES
A DOPE BOY'S QUEEN 3 by ARYANNA

<u>Coming Soon from Lock Down Publications/Ca$h Presents</u>

BLOOD OF A BOSS **VI**

SHADOWS OF THE GAME II

TRAP BASTARD II

By **Askari**

LOYAL TO THE GAME **IV**

By **T.J. & Jelissa**

IF TRUE SAVAGE **VIII**

MIDNIGHT CARTEL IV

DOPE BOY MAGIC IV

CITY OF KINGZ III

NIGHTMARE ON SILENT AVE II

By **Chris Green**

BLAST FOR ME **III**

A SAVAGE DOPEBOY III

CUTTHROAT MAFIA III

DUFFLE BAG CARTEL VII

HEARTLESS GOON VI

By **Ghost**

A HUSTLER'S DECEIT III

KILL ZONE II

BAE BELONGS TO ME III

By **Aryanna**

COKE KINGS V

KING OF THE TRAP III

By **T.J. Edwards**

GORILLAZ IN THE BAY V

3X KRAZY III

De'Kari

KINGPIN KILLAZ IV

STREET KINGS III

PAID IN BLOOD III

CARTEL KILLAZ IV

DOPE GODS III

Hood Rich

SINS OF A HUSTLA II

ASAD

RICH $AVAGE II

By Troublesome

YAYO V

Bred In The Game 2

S. Allen

CREAM III

By Yolanda Moore

SON OF A DOPE FIEND III

HEAVEN GOT A GHETTO II

By Renta

LOYALTY AIN'T PROMISED III

By Keith Williams

I'M NOTHING WITHOUT HIS LOVE II

SINS OF A THUG II

TO THE THUG I LOVED BEFORE II

By Monet Dragun

QUIET MONEY IV

EXTENDED CLIP III

THUG LIFE IV

By **Trai'Quan**

THE STREETS MADE ME IV

By **Larry D. Wright**

IF YOU CROSS ME ONCE II

By **Anthony Fields**

THE STREETS WILL NEVER CLOSE II

By K'ajji

HARD AND RUTHLESS III

Von Diesel

KILLA KOUNTY II

By Khufu

MOBBED UP IV

By King Rio

MONEY GAME II

By Smoove Dolla

A GANGSTA'S KARMA II

By FLAME

JACK BOYZ VERSUS DOPE BOYZ

By Romell Tukes

<u>Available Now</u>

RESTRAINING ORDER **I & II**
By **CA$H & Coffee**
LOVE KNOWS NO BOUNDARIES **I II & III**
By **Coffee**
RAISED AS A GOON I, II, III & IV
BRED BY THE SLUMS I, II, III
BLAST FOR ME I & II
ROTTEN TO THE CORE I II III
A BRONX TALE I, II, III
DUFFLE BAG CARTEL I II III IV V VI
HEARTLESS GOON I II III IV V
A SAVAGE DOPEBOY I II
DRUG LORDS I II III
CUTTHROAT MAFIA I II
KING OF THE TRENCHES
By **Ghost**
LAY IT DOWN **I & II**
LAST OF A DYING BREED I II
BLOOD STAINS OF A SHOTTA I & II III
By **Jamaica**
LOYAL TO THE GAME I II III
LIFE OF SIN I, II III
By **TJ & Jelissa**
BLOODY COMMAS I & II
SKI MASK CARTEL I II & III
KING OF NEW YORK I II,III IV V

RISE TO POWER I II III

COKE KINGS I II III IV

BORN HEARTLESS I II III IV

KING OF THE TRAP I II

By **T.J. Edwards**

IF LOVING HIM IS WRONG...I & II

LOVE ME EVEN WHEN IT HURTS I II III

By **Jelissa**

WHEN THE STREETS CLAP BACK I & II III

THE HEART OF A SAVAGE I II III

By **Jibril Williams**

A DISTINGUISHED THUG STOLE MY HEART I II & III

LOVE SHOULDN'T HURT I II III IV

RENEGADE BOYS I II III IV

PAID IN KARMA I II III

SAVAGE STORMS I II

AN UNFORESEEN LOVE

By **Meesha**

A GANGSTER'S CODE I &, II III

A GANGSTER'S SYN I II III

THE SAVAGE LIFE I II III

CHAINED TO THE STREETS I II III

BLOOD ON THE MONEY I II III

By **J-Blunt**

PUSH IT TO THE LIMIT

By **Bre' Hayes**

BLOOD OF A BOSS **I, II, III, IV, V**

SHADOWS OF THE GAME

TRAP BASTARD

By **Askari**

THE STREETS BLEED MURDER **I, II & III**

THE HEART OF A GANGSTA I II& III

By **Jerry Jackson**

CUM FOR ME I II III IV V VI VII

An **LDP Erotica Collaboration**

BRIDE OF A HUSTLA **I II & II**

THE FETTI GIRLS **I, II& III**

CORRUPTED BY A GANGSTA I, II III, IV

BLINDED BY HIS LOVE

THE PRICE YOU PAY FOR LOVE I, II ,III

DOPE GIRL MAGIC I II III

By **Destiny Skai**

WHEN A GOOD GIRL GOES BAD

By **Adrienne**

THE COST OF LOYALTY I II III

By Kweli

A GANGSTER'S REVENGE **I II III & IV**

THE BOSS MAN'S DAUGHTERS I II III IV V

A SAVAGE LOVE **I & II**

BAE BELONGS TO ME I II

A HUSTLER'S DECEIT I, II, III

WHAT BAD BITCHES DO I, II, III

SOUL OF A MONSTER I II III

KILL ZONE

A DOPE BOY'S QUEEN I II III

By **Aryanna**

A KINGPIN'S AMBITON

A KINGPIN'S AMBITION **II**

I MURDER FOR THE DOUGH

By **Ambitious**

TRUE SAVAGE I II III IV V VI VII

DOPE BOY MAGIC I, II, III

MIDNIGHT CARTEL I II III

CITY OF KINGZ I II

NIGHTMARE ON SILENT AVE

By **Chris Green**

A DOPEBOY'S PRAYER

By **Eddie "Wolf" Lee**

THE KING CARTEL **I, II & III**

By **Frank Gresham**

THESE NIGGAS AIN'T LOYAL **I, II & III**

By **Nikki Tee**

GANGSTA SHYT **I II &III**

By **CATO**

THE ULTIMATE BETRAYAL

By **Phoenix**

BOSS'N UP **I , II & III**

By **Royal Nicole**

I LOVE YOU TO DEATH

By **Destiny J**

I RIDE FOR MY HITTA

I STILL RIDE FOR MY HITTA

By **Misty Holt**

LOVE & CHASIN' PAPER

By **Qay Crockett**

TO DIE IN VAIN

SINS OF A HUSTLA

By **ASAD**

BROOKLYN HUSTLAZ

By **Boogsy Morina**

BROOKLYN ON LOCK I & II

By **Sonovia**

GANGSTA CITY

By **Teddy Duke**

A DRUG KING AND HIS DIAMOND I & II III

A DOPEMAN'S RICHES

HER MAN, MINE'S TOO I, II

CASH MONEY HO'S

THE WIFEY I USED TO BE I II

By Nicole Goosby

TRAPHOUSE KING **I II & III**

KINGPIN KILLAZ I II III

STREET KINGS I II

PAID IN BLOOD **I II**

CARTEL KILLAZ I II III

DOPE GODS I II

By **Hood Rich**

LIPSTICK KILLAH **I, II, III**

CRIME OF PASSION I II & III
FRIEND OR FOE I II III
By **Mimi**
STEADY MOBBN' **I, II, III**
THE STREETS STAINED MY SOUL I II
By **Marcellus Allen**
WHO SHOT YA **I, II, III**
SON OF A DOPE FIEND I II
HEAVEN GOT A GHETTO
Renta
GORILLAZ IN THE BAY **I II III IV**
TEARS OF A GANGSTA I II
3X KRAZY I II
DE'KARI
TRIGGADALE I II III
Elijah R. Freeman
GOD BLESS THE TRAPPERS I, II, III
THESE SCANDALOUS STREETS I, II, III
FEAR MY GANGSTA I, II, III IV, V
THESE STREETS DON'T LOVE NOBODY I, II
BURY ME A G I, II, III, IV, V
A GANGSTA'S EMPIRE I, II, III, IV
THE DOPEMAN'S BODYGAURD I II
THE REALEST KILLAZ I II III
THE LAST OF THE OGS I II III
Tranay Adams
THE STREETS ARE CALLING

Duquie Wilson

MARRIED TO A BOSS I II III

By Destiny Skai & Chris Green

KINGZ OF THE GAME I II III IV V

Playa Ray

SLAUGHTER GANG I II III

RUTHLESS HEART I II III

By Willie Slaughter

FUK SHYT

By Blakk Diamond

DON'T F#CK WITH MY HEART I II

By Linnea

ADDICTED TO THE DRAMA I II III

IN THE ARM OF HIS BOSS II

By Jamila

YAYO I II III IV

A SHOOTER'S AMBITION I II

BRED IN THE GAME

By S. Allen

TRAP GOD I II III

RICH $AVAGE

By Troublesome

FOREVER GANGSTA

GLOCKS ON SATIN SHEETS I II

By Adrian Dulan

TOE TAGZ I II III

LEVELS TO THIS SHYT I II

A Dope Boy's Queen 3

By Ah'Million
KINGPIN DREAMS I II III
By Paper Boi Rari
CONFESSIONS OF A GANGSTA I II III
By Nicholas Lock
I'M NOTHING WITHOUT HIS LOVE
SINS OF A THUG
TO THE THUG I LOVED BEFORE
By Monet Dragun
CAUGHT UP IN THE LIFE I II III
By Robert Baptiste
NEW TO THE GAME I II III
MONEY, MURDER & MEMORIES I II III
By **Malik D. Rice**
LIFE OF A SAVAGE I II III
A GANGSTA'S QUR'AN I II III
MURDA SEASON I II III
GANGLAND CARTEL I II III
CHI'RAQ GANGSTAS I II III
KILLERS ON ELM STREET I II III
JACK BOYZ N DA BRONX I II III
A DOPEBOY'S DREAM
By **Romell Tukes**
LOYALTY AIN'T PROMISED I II
By Keith Williams
QUIET MONEY I II III
THUG LIFE I II III

EXTENDED CLIP I II

By **Trai'Quan**

THE STREETS MADE ME I II III

By **Larry D. Wright**

THE ULTIMATE SACRIFICE I, II, III, IV, V, VI

KHADIFI

IF YOU CROSS ME ONCE

ANGEL I II

IN THE BLINK OF AN EYE

By **Anthony Fields**

THE LIFE OF A HOOD STAR

By **Ca$h & Rashia Wilson**

THE STREETS WILL NEVER CLOSE

By **K'ajji**

CREAM I II

By **Yolanda Moore**

NIGHTMARES OF A HUSTLA I II III

By **King Dream**

CONCRETE KILLA I II

By **Kingpen**

HARD AND RUTHLESS I II

MOB TOWN 251

By **Von Diesel**

GHOST MOB

Stilloan Robinson

MOB TIES I II

By **SayNoMore**

BODYMORE MURDERLAND I II III

By Delmont Player

FOR THE LOVE OF A BOSS

By C. D. Blue

MOBBED UP I II III

By King Rio

KILLA KOUNTY

By Khufu

MONEY GAME

By Smoove Dolla

A GANGSTA'S KARMA

By FLAME

BOOKS BY LDP'S CEO, CA$H

TRUST IN NO MAN

TRUST IN NO MAN 2

TRUST IN NO MAN 3

BONDED BY BLOOD

SHORTY GOT A THUG

THUGS CRY

THUGS CRY 2

THUGS CRY 3

TRUST NO BITCH

TRUST NO BITCH 2

TRUST NO BITCH 3

TIL MY CASKET DROPS

RESTRAINING ORDER

RESTRAINING ORDER 2

IN LOVE WITH A CONVICT

LIFE OF A HOOD STAR

A Dope Boy's Queen 3